DARE TO STAY

Dare Nation Novel #4

NEW YORK TIMES BESTSELLING AUTHOR

Carly Phillips

DARE TO STAY

He's the one who left.
She's the one he left behind.

Willow James, athletic trainer for the Miami Thunder football team, knows abandonment and hurt. A child of foster care, she's been moved around and left behind more times than she cares to count. Just when she was starting to let her guard down with Braden Prescott, he left for a two year stint with Doctors Without Borders. Now he's back.

Dr. Braden Prescott always felt like an outsider in his family of professional sports players. He's traveled the world and is better for it, but now he's home with a job for the Miami Thunder. When he comes face to face with the woman he left behind, their chemistry still smolders. She'll give him her body again but not her heart.

He knows leaving her once was the biggest mistake of his life. Can Willow learn to trust him not to leave, especially when adventure comes calling again?

Chapter One

BRADEN PRESCOTT'S SUIT felt stiff and scratchy, a far cry from the loose scrubs he'd worn for the last two years with Doctors Without Borders. He pulled at the knot on his tie as he waited for the press conference to begin, announcing him as head team general doctor for the Miami Thunder. Beside him was his cousin and team owner, Ian Dare.

"Nervous?" Ian asked, an understanding look on his face.

"More like uncomfortable." And stressed but Braden wasn't about to admit as much. Instead he rolled his shoulders in a futile effort to unwind and believe this new phase would work out.

"Excuse me. I need to talk to someone before the press conference starts." Ian placed a hand on Braden's shoulder before walking away, leaving him to ponder his sudden life change.

It was ironic that he'd accepted this position considering sports medicine had never been on his list of career choices. And for good reason. He'd steered clear of anything that reminded him of the father who'd raised him, because Jesse Prescott had belittled him for his brain, wanting only sons capable of smashing into other men on a football field.

Four of his siblings had ended up in sports in one way or another, and Braden was proud of all they'd accomplished, but it had never been his calling. However, now that he was back in town, he needed a job as much as Ian needed a general practitioner physician he could trust. The last man who'd held the job had betrayed his oath and the people he was supposed to care for.

From the wings, Braden glanced out into the audience of reporters in the front seats and team members filing into the chairs in the back. He caught sight of Hudson Northfield, his best friend, whose idea it had been to join Doctors Without Borders. He'd returned to the States with Braden and come to Florida instead of heading home to New York, where his high-pressured family resided. At Braden's recommendation, Ian had hired Hudson as a team physician, meaning he'd be staying in Florida and not moving home.

But Braden wasn't looking for Hudson when he scanned the crowd. He was searching for a certain blonde-haired, blue-eyed siren he'd left behind. He and Willow James, now head of the Athletic Training Department for the Thunder, had been a couple before Hudson had approached him about joining Doctors Without Border, or MSF as it was known, Médicins Sans Frontières.

He'd been the odd man out at home, the only Prescott brother who hadn't been into sports, and the opportunity to travel and help people in need, while carving out his own niche in life, had been too much of a lure to turn down. At the time, he'd thought Willow, with whom he'd been in an exclusive but not overly serious relationship, would accept the notion that he'd be gone for two years. That they'd see one another when possible. He'd been wrong.

She'd listened, nodded, told him to have a nice life, and walked out, stunning him with how easily she'd dismissed him. Although looking back and knowing her foster care background, he should have dug deeper into her reaction. Instead he'd left despite knowing he'd hurt her with his sudden pronouncement, not taking into consideration the fact that she probably felt abandoned and had thrown up her walls. And though he didn't regret the time he'd spent abroad, he knew he'd done irreparable damage to their relationship.

When Ian had offered him the job, he'd done his research on who he'd be working with, already knowing she'd been with the Thunder when he left. And maybe he'd scanned her social media. A little. The glimpses being the equivalent of a punch in the gut as

3

he realized how much he'd given up when he'd left.

He hadn't realized the depth of his feelings for her until he'd been gone. Hadn't thought he'd miss her as much as he had. And considering her silence in response to his early texts and the calls she'd let go unanswered, she hadn't forgiven him for his last-minute decision to leave.

As the head of the Thunder's Athletic Training Department, she'd be answering to him as lead team physician, something he doubted would make her happy. But they were both adults and professionals. They'd make things work.

And if he had his way, he'd win back her trust.

Somehow.

* * *

WILLOW JAMES WALKED down the hall of the Miami Thunder Football Stadium, headed to the area reserved for press conferences. Ian Dare would be announcing the new head physician. Normally the information would be revealed via press release to the public and in a private team meeting, but given the fact that the former doctor, Peter Jonas, was currently doing time in prison for defrauding the IRS, taking a bribe to pay gambling debts, and injecting the Thunder's star quarterback with banned substances in return for money to pay off his loans, the team needed to make a statement.

As she turned a corner toward the press room, she passed life-size photographs of the Thunder's star players, a tribute that followed them from the old stadium. Because this one was new, the smell of paint still permeated the air around her.

She'd been around the organization for a while, had done two summers and a full-year internship with the team prior to working as one of the trainers for years before being promoted to lead last month. She knew how fortunate she was to have found a place for herself with the Thunder. There were many trainers like her with a stellar academic record, but it had been her relationship with Dr. Peter Jonas, her one-time foster father, that had given her an in. Having known him for years, she'd never suspected he was capable of such betrayal.

His wife, Bella, was destroyed, and since the Jonases were the last of five foster homes Willow had been in, and by then she'd been near to adulthood, she had an ongoing relationship with them, unlike the other families who'd taken her in and easily let her go. She kept in close touch with Bella and spoke to her often. If there was anyone in her life Willow trusted, it was Bella Jonas, and she'd look out for her any way she had to.

Peter was another person who'd let her down. Life

taught her that it was in her best interest to keep people at a distance, and every time she broke that rule, she'd been hurt in the end.

Given Damon Prescott's status, the news about Doc had spread fast, hitting the team hard. Ian had withheld the name of the new doctor until announcement time, and she'd find out along with everyone else in a few minutes.

She stepped into the room, the crowd of reporters buzzing with anticipation over the upcoming news. Scanning the seats in the back, she walked toward the closest person to her in the Athletic Training Department, Steffy Hughes, a petite brunette who was a few years younger than Willow's thirty-one. But they'd been friends for almost two years, shared drinks after work, attended exercise classes together, and bonded over their love of sports. As the only two women in the training department, they'd gravitated toward each other, and Willow had let Steffy in more than she did most people.

"Glad I'm not late. I was doing paperwork and lost track of time," Willow said as she slid in beside her friend.

Steffy shook her head. "Not at all. Any ideas who they're bringing on?"

"Not a clue. I haven't heard of any shake-ups at other teams, so they're not grabbing anyone we'd know of that way. I just know that Mr. Dare wants to make a statement that we're starting fresh and with someone who has no possibility of being corrupted in any way. He hated the scandal that hit us."

"Didn't we all," Steffy said. "Everyone has been tiptoeing around here. I'm ready for a change in atmosphere. I know Doc's second in charge has been holding down the fort, but everyone knows he's looking to move west with his family. We're mid-season and need a qualified doctor in charge."

"Amen," Willow said, just as Ian Dare strode into the room and stood at the podium.

An imposing man in a black suit with a white shirt, top button opened, Ian was also extremely good-looking. He exuded power by virtue of his attitude and backed up his controlling demeanor with a solid work ethic, so everyone respected him. With his dark brown hair and very familiar indigo eyes, every time she saw Ian, she was reminded of the man she wanted to forget.

The man she'd dubbed *he who shall not be named.* The well-known words fit the guy who'd easily dumped her and taken off for parts unknown. Ironically, *he* was also related to Ian, information that had come to light after he'd left for a stint with Doctors Without Borders. A decision he'd made seemingly out of nowhere.

Not that they'd been looking toward the future, but she'd had strong feelings for him that had been growing by the day. She'd let herself start to fall for him despite knowing better, and she'd thought she knew what his plans were and had foolishly let herself believe they'd included her. Just another time in her life she'd been let down and left behind. Something she would not let happen again.

"Welcome and thank you for joining me here today along with Coach Carson." Ian gestured to the man beside him who ran the team before going into a long speech about the integrity of the Miami Thunder organization and everyone who worked for and was associated with them.

She'd zoned out for a few minutes when clapping around her alerted her to the fact that she'd missed something important.

Shaking her head, she looked up and watched in shock as *he* strode onto the stage. Dr. Braden Prescott. The man who'd walked out on her two years ago and apparently the new head physician for the Miami Thunder.

Her heart pounded so hard in her chest she heard the sound in her ears. He looked scrumptious in his dark suit and the short scruff of beard he hadn't had last time she saw him. As if no time had passed, her traitorous body responded to his presence.

"Oh my God, he's hot," Steffy said, waving her hand in front of her face at the same time Willow spoke. "Oh, shit, that's my ex."

"What?" Steffy asked too loudly, then lowered her voice. "You were with that gorgeous guy?" Steffy had been hired not long after Braden left, and Willow had already locked up her feelings and closed them in a box in her mind, never to be opened again.

Willow nodded. "We were together for a year, but I haven't seen him in two."

"Well, you'll be working with him now. Oh no! What will Cole think?" Steffy asked of the doctor on staff Willow was currently dating.

Her stomach twisted at the thought. She and Cole Walsh had just started going out. She was keeping things casual, and he respected her need to go slow. She hadn't slept with anyone since Braden because she hadn't met any man who made her want to allow him that close. She thought Cole had potential. Now she had Braden to contend with, although given how easily he'd taken off, she doubted he'd be interested in her now. And she wasn't into second chances after being left.

"Your life suddenly got complicated," Steffy muttered.

No shit, she thought.

"Can you handle it?" her friend asked.

"Doesn't look like I have a choice." Willow glanced at the podium once more and realized Braden was staring directly at her.

As he stood next to his cousin, the family resemblance was clear. Dark hair, strong jaw, full lips... She even remembered how good he smelled, the scent of his woodsy cologne, and the feel of his body against hers. She closed her eyes and wondered how in the fresh hell this had happened. The man she'd spent two years trying to forget would now be permanently in her orbit?

She grabbed her phone and whispered, "I'm going to get ready for my next patient." It was a lie. She didn't have anyone on schedule, and Steffy probably knew it.

But she needed to get out of this room full of people and hole up in her office, where she could catch her breath and shore up her defenses against Braden Prescott, MD.

* * *

BRADEN WATCHED WILLOW stand up and walk out the side door of the press room, and his sole goal was to get through this conference and find her. He'd noted the shock in her expression upon seeing him and kicked himself for not warning her ahead of time. Not that she'd have taken his call, but he could have texted or left a message.

She looked beautiful, her blonde hair tied in a ponytail, her face lightly made up. He couldn't see what she wore besides the black long-sleeve workout top that clung to her curves. If he had any doubt about his feelings, if he'd wondered whether time was making him long for someone and seeing her would shake him out of his stupor, he now knew.

He wanted her back.

Forcing himself to focus, he answered questions about his background. Discussed how he'd finished college early, fast-tracked med school and his residency, worked at a clinic downtown, then done his stint with MSF. He was also board-certified in sports medicine, something he'd done because of his brothers' career choices. He wanted to be available if needed. Now he was home and ready for the opportunity to head the team.

Had family strings been pulled in his hiring? Ian had answered that question. Probably but Ian was adamant that Braden was trustworthy and that mattered when his team had been shattered by Dr. Jonas's betrayal. He'd ended questions there.

Braden strode off the stage, determined to see Willow, only to be waylaid by team members wanting to welcome him, and he had to take time for the introductions and conversations with the people he'd be working with in the upcoming days and weeks. They needed to get to know and trust him with their bodies and injuries, and he wouldn't shirk those responsibilities in favor of his love life.

"Good job!" a familiar voice said with warmth and excitement.

"Brianne!" He turned to face his twin with a grin, extremely happy to see her.

Being away from his family had been difficult. Being separated from his twin sister had been twice as hard. He and Bri had a bond no one but them could really understand. Since he'd been home, she'd been busy with clients and planning their brother Jaxon's wedding, while he'd been organizing his new life, renting an apartment, and conducting meetings with Ian about this job.

"I couldn't miss my brother's big introduction." She pulled him into a tight hug. "I'm so glad you're back, and I know you're going to kick ass at this position."

She stepped back and tucked her dark hair behind one ear. "Okay, why do you look stressed? Is this too much for you?" She gestured around the room still full of people.

He shook his head. "I'm fine. There's just someone I need to see, and I haven't had a second to slip out of here."

"Aah. Willow?"

He inclined his head. "Willow."

Bri had known Willow from the year that she and Braden had been involved. She was a publicist at their brother Austin's firm, Dare Nation, and many of her clients were Thunder players, so she kept up with staffing and roster changes. She'd know that Willow was now head of the Athletic Training Department. The two women had gotten along well, but Willow tended to keep people at a distance, and Bri had respected her boundaries. Braden had just begun to break through her outer shell to the soft woman beneath when the MSF opportunity had come up.

"You're distracted. Come. I'll walk with you to the training area, then I'll go bother some of my clients about their lack of social media presence."

He chuckled. "I wouldn't want to be them."

Bri was the best at what she did, because before she took on a client, she laid out exactly what she both needed and expected of them. Once they agreed, she rode them hard to get the optimal result, but that could make her a pain in the ass, which was what they paid her to be.

She nudged Braden in the ribs. "They love me."

He rolled his eyes just as Hudson walked up and joined them. "Good job," he said, slapping Braden on the back.

"I was just telling him that," Bri said.

Hudson smiled at Bri. "You look beautiful today. The royal blue in your shirt brings out your eyes."

"Is that your way of flirting?" Bri asked, sounding almost coy.

Braden narrowed his gaze. "I think it was a compliment. I'm not so sure he'd make a play in front of your brother. Your *twin*."

That earned him another nudge in his ribs. "I don't need you protecting me like I'm five years old."

Hudson laughed. "You two bicker like siblings. I'm complimenting a beautiful woman. Although if I wanted to date her, I'd think you'd approve of your best friend asking your sister out?" Hudson threw the volley back and smiled at them both. "See you later," he said, and before Braden could reply, he strode off, shaking his head.

"You made me look like I can't handle myself. Like a child. Don't do that," Bri said, obviously annoyed with him.

He held up both hands. "I'm sorry. Hudson's a good guy. It was just instinct to protect you."

"Well, as I tell my four brothers, I don't need protection!"

"I'll always look out for you," Braden said, being deliberately stubborn because it was true.

She let out an exasperated noise. "How about we

go find Willow and put your love life front and center?" she asked, clearly still worked up over his interference.

"Sounds like a plan," he muttered.

They headed out of the room, and although Ian had given him a tour of the stadium during off hours, he was glad to have Bri by his side directing him. Even if she was still annoyed with him.

After passing through the Hall of Fame, which included Austin, who had retired as a wide receiver, he thought maybe one day Damon, the current quarterback, would also hang on these hallowed walls.

Bri stopped at a point where they could go straight or right. "Since I doubt you want to face her for the first time with your sister holding your hand, I'll leave you here. Down that hall and the room on the right. Her name's on the door."

"Come on, Bri. Don't be mad at me." He used his most cajoling voice.

She frowned but he could tell it was forced. "I'm not mad. You're just annoying."

"But you love me." He kissed her cheek. "Talk to you soon."

He turned and headed down the hall, scanning the doors with name plaques on each. He realized from his previous tour that Willow's office probably connected on another side to the gym area where the trainers worked with the athletes.

Drawing a deep breath, he knocked on her door.

*   *   *

WILLOW RETURNED TO her office and tried to immerse herself in the information on her computer about current players and their injuries but kept spacing out. She found it hard to focus when all she could see was Braden standing on the stage, looking so good in his suit and new scruff of beard. She hated how her body still responded to a mere look at him.

She clicked on the mouse of her computer when a knock sounded on her door, no doubt Steffy coming by to gossip about her blurting out her past relationship with the team's new doctor.

"Come in!" she called out. She closed out the page she was looking at and glanced up as her door opened and Braden walked inside, shutting the door behind him. Her stomach flipped at the sight of him, and she rose to her feet.

"Willow, it's really good to see you." He stepped toward her, his arms out, clearly intending to hug her. Being in his embrace and inhaling his sexy scent was the last thing she could handle, and she held out a hand to stop him from coming any closer.

He stopped, respecting her boundaries, and she let out a sigh of relief. "How are you, Braden?"

"I'm good. Settling in. How have you been?" he asked, those violet eyes staring into hers.

"Also good. Enjoying my promotion, which reminds me. Congratulations on your new position." She folded her arms across her chest in an effort to keep a barrier between them.

"Thank you. I'm looking forward to getting to know everyone and traveling with the team."

God, she hadn't let herself think about the fact that they'd be on away trips together, as well.

"You look great," he said, his gaze taking her in, and though she wore a pair of black leggings and a Thunder fitted shirt, she felt naked beneath his stare.

"Thanks." She didn't want things to get personal nor did she desire a conversation about when he had returned or how his time with MSF had been. "So what can I do for you?"

"First, I wanted to say hello. Second, we'll be working together, and I thought we should clear the air."

She inclined her head. "Don't worry. My entire staff will keep you up-to-date on every player." She turned away from him and stepped toward her desk, away from the scent of his cologne that would now linger in her personal space.

He groaned and ran a hand through his hair, messing it in ways she'd seen when they'd finished a round in bed. Clearing her throat, she sat down in her chair, hoping he'd take it as a dismissal.

"Willow, look. I'm sorry about how things ended between us and I'd like to talk." He strode closer to her desk.

"There's nothing to discuss unless it's about the team." She answered before he could settle himself on the corner as he'd clearly been about to do. "We're colleagues and I'll be professional. I'll talk to you when I need to, and nothing will fall through the cracks, but I want to be clear. There is nothing personal between us. Not anymore." Resting her hands on her lap, she curled them into fists, her nails digging into her skin.

This conversation was costing her. Her pulse was racing and her stomach churning. She resented the fact that this man could still have a hold over her in any way.

"That's where you're wrong." He grasped the arm of her chair and spun her to face him, then braced his hands behind her shoulders.

His face was close to hers, his lips so near if she moved at all she'd be kissing him.

"I can see the emotion you're holding back," he said in a deep voice. "We have unresolved issues, and you can be sure we'll be discussing them. In the meantime, how about a tour of the place?"

She narrowed her gaze. "Didn't Ian walk you

through the stadium when he was trying to sway you to take this job?"

"I have a bad sense of direction. I need another one." He stood up straight, and she could breathe now that they weren't face-to-face. He was still too close for comfort, she thought, as she rolled her eyes at his blatant lie. They both knew he had an excellent sense of direction.

"I would also like you to run me through the daily schedule and fill me in on anything I need to know from your perspective so I can hit the ground running. I know the team is home this weekend, but we have an away game the weekend after. Anything you can clarify for me will be great."

"Fine." She couldn't say no to his request, so she cleared her throat and waited for him to get the message and step out of her personal space.

Once he did, she held back the sigh of relief and pushed herself to her feet. "I'll show you around, and then we can go over the players who are possibly on the IRL. Injured Reserve List, in case you don't know."

"I did grow up in a sports-centered house. I'm aware of the terms. Just let me leave my jacket here. I can't stand how stuffy I feel." He shrugged off the jacket and, to her surprise, tugged at his tie next.

"What are you doing?"

"Relaxing now that the press conference is over." He pulled at his tie, loosening it, then undoing it completely, and to her frustration, undid two buttons on his shirt, revealing the sprinkling of dark chest hair she used to lay her hand on after always amazing sex.

Shit, shit, shit. She had to stop thinking of the past.

He laid the jacket over the arm of her chair and added his tie on top.

"Ready?" she asked, trying not to show how much he affected her.

"Sure am." He grinned as if he could absolutely read her mind and winked.

She shivered and hoped he didn't notice her hardening nipples. The damned man. "Then let's go."

He gestured to the door. "Ladies first."

He always had been a gentleman. She stepped ahead of him, feeling the burn of his stare on her back as she walked out of the room.

Chapter Two

"WHAT TIME DO you get to work in the morning?" Braden asked Willow as she gave him a tour of the facility, doing his best to keep his gaze off her sweet behind as he followed her around.

Instead he'd listened carefully to the information she gave him and focused when she introduced him to people he hadn't yet met. Ian planned a team gathering for later in the day where Braden would get to know everyone better.

"This way to the gym," she said, turning a corner as she answered. "I'm in the office by four forty-five a.m. and in the gym by five thirty to start treatments. I go through therapeutic modalities, like ultrasound, joint mobilization techniques, soft tissue massage, stretching, exercise, and the like."

He nodded, knowing the hours he'd have to be here during the season. "Tough schedule," he said.

"You get used to it."

They entered the state-of-the-art workout room, where athletes were on various pieces of equipment, other trainers stretching and working with the players.

Not only did he take mental notes for himself during this tour, he watched Willow deal with the people on her training team, the other physicians, and the players, admiring the mix of professional and joking relationships she had.

Seeing her in her work environment was a revelation. He'd only known her one-on-one or interacting with friends as a couple. On a personal level, she was often reticent to give out much information about herself, but here was different. It was obvious the guys respected her, trusted her judgment, and genuinely liked her as a person, causing Braden's admiration for her to grow.

He was well aware of the wall she'd put up between them, and he took her warning that they were over seriously. But he interpreted her reactions differently than her words. Hearing the stiffness in her voice and seeing the way she wouldn't relax and talk to him told him there were still feelings that ran deep. If she didn't care, she wouldn't be holding in so much hurt. As much as he hated knowing he'd caused that pain, he hoped to work their way through it.

Call him an optimist but he wasn't giving up. He now had time and space to repair their relationship.

"Hey, it's my brother!" Damon's voice rang out in the room.

Braden turned in time to see his sibling stride away from the weights he'd been lifting and walk over to him.

Damon slapped him on the back. "Welcome to the team." He glanced from Braden to Willow and back again, his curiosity obviously piqued.

Braden held his breath, hoping his brother wouldn't say something that would make her uncomfortable in front of the guys. Something about their past relationship.

"Has Willow been showing you the ropes?" Damon asked, and Braden released a long whoosh of air.

"He's going to have to catch up quickly. We're on the clock. Game in six days," she said in her proficient voice.

The one she'd been using with him for the last half hour as opposed to her sultry voice, the one he heard in his dreams. "I can handle it," he assured her.

"It's not like he was in a cushy place before this," Damon said. "I think he'll do all right." He grinned. "Gotta get back to work. Evie said to invite you for dinner one night soon."

"Name the night and I'll be there." He wanted to get to know his brother's wife and become closer to all of their significant others.

Damon strode off and Braden turned to Willow. "What's next?"

"Tour's over," she said. "But I'm always around if you have questions about the players or the schedule."

Holding back his groan because he wasn't ready to end his time with her, he merely nodded. "I appreciate you showing me around. I know you're busy."

"It's fine. We're a team here. Ready to head back? Your jacket's in my office," she said, obviously eager to get rid of him.

He wasn't about to let her get away that easily. "Sure." He walked to the entrance of the gym and pushed the door open for her, following her out. His plan was to invite her to dinner so they could catch up and, he hoped, dig deeper than the surface conversation she'd allowed today.

They stepped back into her office, and once again he was in close quarters with Willow, surrounded by the delicious scent of coconut, his favorite smell since she'd always favored that in shower gel and shampoo. All he had to do was inhale and his cock stood at attention, which gave him a reason to shrug his jacket back on and cover the evidence of his arousal.

Had he been with other women in the last two years? Yes. Did he remember faces or names? No. And he'd always thought of Willow and wished it was her he was with.

"So I was wondering," he began, intending to ask her if they could get together, as a knock sounded on the open door.

Not ready to share her yet, Braden turned to see who needed her attention. A man he didn't recognize stood in the doorway. A blond-haired, brown-eyed, well-groomed guy wearing khakis and a short-sleeve Polo shirt.

"Am I interrupting?" the man asked.

Willow blinked, a flush on her cheeks. "No, of course not. Braden Prescott, this is Cole Walsh, one of the team physicians. You'll be working together."

Stepping forward, Braden extended his arm and they shook hands.

"My new boss." The man took Braden in, obviously sizing him up, and Braden did the same.

"Good to meet you and looking forward to working with you," Cole said at last.

"Same here. I'll be announcing an official meeting in the morning, after I've been introduced to everyone this afternoon," Braden said.

"Great." Cole smiled and turned to Willow. "Are you ready for lunch? I know we don't have much time, but I made a reservation at your favorite place." His expression as he turned to her was of a man smitten.

That flush in her cheeks deepened as she looked at Braden beneath lowered lashes before glancing at Cole. "Sounds perfect. We're finished here, right, Braden?" Without waiting for a reply, she opened a drawer in her desk and picked up her handbag.

Shit. She was with another man, one he'd be working with. That was a hiccup he hadn't anticipated, and jealousy rose fast and furious inside him.

"Have fun," he said as she walked past him without meeting his gaze.

Son of a bitch. Now what?

*   *   *

"SO I GAVE him a tour and we went back to my office and Cole interrupted and he and I went to lunch." Willow took a sip of the wine she'd poured for both herself and Steffy, who'd stopped by on her way home after work.

When Steffy was hired, she'd also been looking for an apartment, and there had been one available in Willow's building, so she'd mentioned the rental. Steffy had liked the area and the unit and rented it immediately. After they'd become friends, she'd often stop by Willow's for a drink and a chat and vice versa.

"Hmm." Steffy settled into the plush sofa in Willow's living room.

"Hmm what?"

She shrugged. "Just hmm. And how was lunch with Cole?"

Willow glanced at her friend over the rim of her glass, taking another sip before answering. "I don't know. I was distracted."

"By a certain hot doctor? And not the one you went to lunch with?" Her friend gave her a knowing look.

"Maybe." Willow blushed at the admission, hating that Braden had the ability to get to her on any level. "But only because I was in shock that he showed up again and I'll be working with him, not because I still have feelings for the man."

"Of course not." Steffy walked into the kitchen, which was a pass-through from the family room, and poured herself more wine.

"You sound like you don't believe me," Willow muttered, knowing her friend was right but unwilling to admit it.

"Oh, that's because I don't. I saw the look on your face during that press conference, and it wasn't just shock. You were drooling." Returning from the kitchen, she settled onto the other end of the couch, tucking a leg beneath her.

Willow rolled her eyes. "I was not drooling." Salivating was more like it, and she hated herself for still being attracted to Braden, never mind letting him ruin her lunch with a perfectly nice man.

"Does Cole know your history with Braden?" Steffy raised an eyebrow in question, and Willow's grip on her wineglass tightened.

She shook her head. "No. I really want to keep my past out of the workplace. Cole and I don't make a public display, and there's no whispers about us. I'd like to keep it that way."

"Which I understand. But that has nothing to do with telling the man you're dating that the new doctor is your ex."

She placed her drink on a coaster on the table and groaned. "It's not an exclusive relationship. I really don't think it's a good idea to mention it and have that kind of mess between the three of us at work."

Steffy narrowed her gaze. "So it's not serious. And you couldn't focus on him at lunch. You're not sleeping with him! How long have you two been dating?" she asked.

"Casually for three months."

"Well, if you haven't slept with him before now, I can guarantee you won't now that Dr. Hottie is back."

She frowned at her friend, but again, Willow wasn't about to admit Steffy had a point. Willow had been holding off taking that next step with him, and Steffy was right. Now she'd been reminded of what she was missing and why she hadn't gone further with Cole.

None of that meant she was interested in rekindling things with Braden, who she could not trust.

*   *   *

THE FIRST WEEK passed quickly, with Braden getting to know the players and the staff. He discovered he enjoyed the hectic pace of the season, keeping up with each man on the team and their chronic issues and those things that put them on the Injured Reserve List. He actually liked the job more than he'd thought he would, coming off humanitarian work.

Seeing Willow every day was a bonus, even if she treated him to her cool, professional persona that didn't give him any way to break through her reserve. He didn't think anyone noticed that they weren't actually speaking to one another. Only Hudson had caught on quickly, but he knew their history. It was only a matter of time before Willow's stiffness around him became obvious to others.

Today was Tuesday and the weekend on the road was fast approaching. He planned to travel with the team and be there on the sidelines. He didn't believe in passing the buck, and though he had other general practitioners who could go, he wanted to show he had the chops for the job, not just Ian's approval.

Dr. Daniel Barrett, head orthopedic surgeon for the team, had two orthopedists and one surgeon traveling with them, and Braden had tapped another GP to go with them. He hadn't chosen Cole Walsh. He'd like to say he wasn't biased against the man or that he didn't want an open road to Willow, but that would be bullshit and he was man enough to admit it. By the same token, he wasn't taking Hudson, either, because two new doctors who didn't know the ropes wouldn't be smart. He understood he needed to learn on the job and watch the people who'd been around longer than him for protocol. But once and if an injury occurred, his instincts would kick in, and he'd know exactly what to do.

Today was the day the coaches put together game plans, and the rookies had been in the gym working out while injured players were being seen by trainers. Braden spent the day examining various guys, eager to get to know them, and by seven p.m., he was exhausted and ready to get out of here.

But he wasn't headed straight to the parking lot. He had a pit stop to make first. He'd taken note of what time Willow called it a day, and tonight he was leaving around the same time and hoped to intercept her before she left.

With a little luck, this time there wouldn't be any interruptions. A certain doctor was working with a particularly tricky patient, and that should keep the man busy, because Braden had a plan.

He headed directly to Willow's office around the corner from his and stopped in the open doorway, catching Willow mid-stretch. Wearing the type of clothing she favored, fitted black leggings and a body-hugging top, she touched her toes, and her sweet, pert ass teased him.

He couldn't contain a groan as his cock responded to her position.

She jerked her body up and swayed from the sudden movement. He reached out and grabbed her, pulling her close to steady her. The warm scent went straight to his already hard groin.

"Thank you but I'm fine now," she said, quickly stepping away. "I didn't realize my office door was open."

He cleared his throat and hoped the desire she'd triggered didn't show on his face. He also prayed she didn't glance down, because the effect she had on him would be glaringly evident.

"What are you doing here?" she asked, gathering up her bag and things to take home for the night.

He met her gaze, her blue eyes narrowed warily. "I came to convince you to have dinner with me. I want to talk and clear the air." And hopefully put the past behind them.

She shook her head. "Not only is it not a good idea but it's unnecessary. We're making do just fine."

"I disagree. You're not speaking to me unless it's about a patient, you're not relaxed around me like you are around everyone else, and we're both traveling to Denver this weekend. So we're going for dinner."

She hesitated, then seemed to come to some sort of conclusion and nodded. "Fine. But somewhere close to my place and I want to be home early. I have to wake up at four thirty."

He'd take that as a win. "Fine by me. Do you still live in the same apartment?"

She nodded.

"And is your favorite Mexican place still around the corner?"

He caught the widening of her eyes. "Yes, I remembered," he said in a gruffer voice than usual. There were many things he recalled about Willow that would surprise her. But there was time to get into that. "Are you ready?"

She nodded, but from her stiff demeanor, it was clear she didn't want to join him for dinner. He was serious when he said it would be good for the team. They needed to work together without resentment getting between them.

"Let's go and I'll follow you there." He wished he could get her alone in his car just to have her near, but he knew she drove to work. They were stuck with two vehicles.

She stepped past him and walked out of the room. Once he joined her, she locked her office, and they headed to the parking lot in silence.

He had questions about her life, but he was saving

them for the restaurant, where nobody they knew would disturb them.

* * *

WILLOW SLID INTO a booth at El Toro and placed her purse between her outer thigh and the wall. Before she could process his intention, Braden slipped in next to her, the warmth of his big body pressing against hers.

"What are you doing? Go sit across from me," she said, inching away because everything about him was so powerful and overwhelming.

He slung one arm behind her and turned her way. "This is my seat, remember? We'd share our guac and chips sitting side by side."

"That was the past."

"And this is the present."

Before she could reply, a waitress stopped at their table. "Can I get you something to drink?"

Willow was going to need one to get through this meal. "A margarita, please."

"Whatever beer you have on tap," Braden said. "And can you please bring guacamole and chips when you get a chance?"

"Of course." The brunette smiled at them. "I'll be back to take the rest of your order," she said and stopped at another table.

Left alone again, Braden turned back to her. "So

how am I doing at work?"

Willow blinked in surprise. "You want my assessment?"

He nodded. "I value your opinion and you've been around the team for years. So let me have it."

She bit down on her lower lip and, for the first time since his arrival, allowed herself to really think about Braden and his first week with the team. He'd blended in seamlessly, the other doctors and therapists deferring to his expertise when necessary. By the same token, he had no problem handing off a player to another doctor if the injury fell under their specialty. He listened and learned the procedure and protocol and asked when he wasn't sure instead of charging in and giving orders.

Even Cole had mentioned to her how much he liked the team's new head doctor. Of course, he wouldn't feel the same way if he knew she had history with Braden, but that was irrelevant to Braden's question.

So as much as she wanted to tell him he'd done a shitty job, she couldn't. "You seem to be fitting in well, actually. No criticism from me."

"I'm glad you think so. Your opinion means a lot to me." His grin was so hot, gave him such a sexy look, she'd be shocked if it hadn't incinerated her panties, and she squirmed in her seat.

"Here are your drinks." Their server returned and placed Willow's glass down, then Braden's bottle on the table in front of him. "Can I take your orders?"

"We haven't had a chance to look at the menu." He glanced at Willow. "Has it changed?"

"No. I'll have the pulled pork soft tacos. Thank you," she said to the server.

"An enchilada for me, thanks." He ordered his usual choice from when they used to come here as a couple.

Their server picked up the unopened menus and walked away.

Not wanting to sit in uncomfortable silence, Willow decided to start their conversation. "So … how has the adjustment been from being abroad to being home?"

He shrugged. "Not bad. I'm renting an apartment in the same building as Hudson. I treated myself to a new bed, and I have to say it's been great to be comfortable again. Cots in tents were hard on my back."

"Are you glad you went?" As soon as the question was out, she wished she could take it back. She didn't want him to know she wondered if he had any regrets.

He met her gaze, his expression somber. "I'm grateful for the experience," he said, obviously speaking with care. "I wish I'd handled certain things differently. Like us."

"It's in the past," she said, wishing she didn't have to keep repeating the refrain.

"Except you're still hurt and angry." He lifted a hand and dropped it again.

She knew from their history what he'd intended. He'd liked to play with her hair, and she'd enjoyed it, too. He'd curl a strand around his finger and tug lightly. The sensation would start in her scalp, but she'd inevitably feel the pull between her thighs. She was glad he'd cut off the impulse. She didn't want to make a scene.

"I *was* hurt," she admitted. "And I was angry. But I'm fine now. We can work together without an issue."

"I'll take your word for it, then."

"Here's your guacamole and chips," the waitress said, returning to place their appetizers on the table.

"Thank you," they both said at the same time.

"I'm starving." Having rushed through a yogurt for lunch and barely having time for half a protein bar later in the afternoon, she needed food.

She reached out and picked up a chip, dipped it in the creamy avocado mix, and took a bite, the salty flavor exploding on her tongue. "Mmm. So good," she moaned at the taste.

His gaze locked on hers. "Do not make that sound around me unless you're prepared for what happens next."

She widened her eyes, shocked at both his gruff tone and the words he'd spoken. Until now he'd been careful around her. Tiptoeing and trying to respect her feelings if not giving her her space. Before she could even process the boundary he'd crossed, he asked, "So what's the story with you and Cole Walsh? Is it serious?" And he crossed another one.

"That's none of your business," she said, refusing to discuss her relationships with him.

"I'll take that as a no, then." Sounding pleased, he picked up a chip, dipped it, and took a bite, leaving her to grind her teeth in frustration because he'd boxed her into a corner.

If she agreed, he'd up his game and come on stronger. Not that she had any idea what it was he wanted from her, but he was obviously still interested. If she disagreed with him, she'd send out all the wrong signals that might get back to Cole, and she didn't want him to get the incorrect idea about their relationship. She enjoyed her time with Cole, but it wasn't serious.

"You're frustrating," she muttered, scooping up guac with another chip, then following it with her first sip of her drink.

He winked and lifted his beer.

Ignoring the flutter in her stomach, she concentrated on the food in front of her instead of the man beside her.

The waitress served their meals, and Braden behaved for the rest of dinner. They talked about various topics, and to her relief, they both veered away from anything too personal.

Instead he caught her up on his family's weddings and engagements.

Jaxon, his baseball-playing brother had ended up in a marriage of convenience with his sister's best friend, Macy. They'd both had strong reasons to marry and ended up falling in love. Damon married the private investigator who had cleared him of the steroid use accusation and discovered Doc's complicity, something she'd heard about at work. And Austin had found a baby on his doorstep and called his assistant, Quinn, in to help. The baby had been his, the mother signed over her rights, not without a lot of drama, and he and Quinn were due to marry on Valentine's Day.

"So all your brothers are married or getting married," she mused aloud.

He nodded. "Just Bri and I are left." He shook his head. "Maybe it's a twin thing and it'll happen around the same time."

She did her best not to react to his offhanded comment. The fact that she'd once, almost, let herself dream about a lifetime with him only for him to drop the Doctors Without Borders bomb on her without warning was, as she'd said, in the past. If his future held a wedding with someone else, so be it, she thought, ignoring the cramping in her stomach at the notion.

* * *

BRADEN CONSIDERED THIS dinner the equivalent of a touchdown. It wasn't a Super Bowl win, but it was another step toward his ultimate goal. He might not be the sports guy in the family, but he could use analogies with the best of them. Just knowing Willow wasn't serious with another man gave him breathing room.

The server put the check on the table, and at Willow's hand movement, he shot her a narrow-eyed warning. Though she frowned, she allowed him to grab the check and pay.

He walked her out to her car and paused before she opened the door. "That wasn't so bad, was it?" he asked of their time together.

"No. It was actually … nice." She pulled her bottom lip between her teeth before releasing it, and he stifled a groan, wishing he could taste her mouth.

But he'd already resigned himself to a slow and steady pursuit and drew a deep breath to calm himself down. He'd fucked things up, and now he had to go at her pace. It was a road worth traveling. One she didn't even realize they were on.

So as much as he wanted to pull her into a long, deep kiss, he'd play it slow. "I'll see you at work tomorrow?"

She nodded. "Bright and early."

Unable to let her leave without a meaningful moment between them, he reached out, winding a lock of hair around his finger, tugging on the strand before releasing it.

Her eyes flew to his and glazed over in a look he remembered well. One that told him the desire he was feeling wasn't one-sided.

Taking advantage, he slid his hand around the back of her neck, pulled her close, and kissed her cheek. "Night, Willow," he whispered into her ear, then stepped back.

Her body trembled and she glanced down, immediately fumbling inside her bag for her keys. Satisfied with her reaction, he waited for her to unlock her car and slide into the driver's seat.

"Thanks for dinner, Braden. Good night," she said, her voice huskier than he'd heard it since his return.

He closed the door, hearing the click of the lock, and he waited until she pulled out before walking to his vehicle.

She might try and go back to professional Willow tomorrow, but he had the satisfaction of knowing he'd broken through her reserve.

Chapter Three

WILLOW HAD A bag she kept packed for away games. One stuffed with toiletries, extra black leggings, and anything else she always needed. It paid to have double and never forget anything. Now she added more items for the weekend into her carry-on. She'd learned at a young age to stay packed in case a social worker arrived to announce she was leaving and going to another family, and since she'd had very few possessions, traveling light came naturally to her. You couldn't fit much in a black trash bag.

Pushing her childhood to the back of her mind, she focused on the weekend ahead, running through her players, injuries, and who'd need pregame preparation. During all of this, she did her best not to think about her dinner with Braden earlier in the week.

Here it was Saturday and she couldn't shake him. He invaded her thoughts constantly. The heat of his body beside hers at the table. The husky tone of his voice. The way he'd twirled her hair like old times, then leaned into her, his cologne a complete turn-on. Her breath had caught as she'd prepared herself for a kiss, only to end up with his lips on her cheek and his gruff voice in her ear.

She shivered at the memory, her nipples tightening as they had that night. Ignoring the sensations wasn't easy, but she did her best, zipping her suitcase and getting ready for work.

She headed to the stadium, where she would join the team on the bus to the airport. A private jet would carry everyone to Denver, and then the rush would begin.

As she walked inside, dragging her bag behind her, Cole caught up with her, jogging from the parking lot. "Hey!" he said, coming up beside her. "Ready to go, I see."

She nodded.

"I'm sitting this one out," he said, and she was unable to read his feelings on the matter. "I promised Joel Clarkson I'd take another look at his knee before you go, so I'm here today anyway."

Having seen the list of doctors who would be at the game, she already knew he was staying behind and wondered if Braden had made that call on purpose. To keep them apart. If so, it was ridiculous. She was all business on these trips.

"I'm sorry to hear that. I'm sure you'll go to the next one." She didn't know what else to say.

He shrugged. "Braden seems fair. He took who he

needed. I'm fine."

She did her best not to wince, because she wasn't certain that was true. She now realized that at some point she was going to have to reveal her history with Braden. It was only fair Cole knew what he might be up against with his new boss. First she'd see what information she could get out of Braden, like whether he'd deliberately left Cole home, and try and make sure he didn't pull that kind of maneuver again.

"I'll miss you. We haven't gotten together in a while outside of a rushed lunch here and there," Cole said, walking her to her office.

"I know. It's been crazy busy." But she knew that was an excuse.

She couldn't put off taking that next step with him much longer, and if she'd been waffling on whether or not to sleep with him before Braden's return, she knew for sure she didn't want to now. Not that she'd be diving into bed with Braden any time soon, but the difference in her feelings for the men was obvious. Which told her that, as hard as she'd tried, she couldn't see herself developing deeper feelings for Cole, and she would have to tell him that soon. But not the day she was leaving for a long weekend.

She reached her office, unlocked the door, and Cole joined her inside. She tucked her carry-on against the wall and was about to sit down at her desk when he grasped her hands.

"So promise me you'll make time for us when you get back?"

She looked into his brown eyes and forced a smile. Yes, they would talk on her return, she thought. He deserved as much. He deserved better than a woman who couldn't reciprocate his feelings.

"Knock knock," a familiar male voice said before she could answer. "Am I interrupting something?"

Dammit, Braden. Did the man have radar? She stepped away from Cole, not that she had been going to kiss him, but Braden had walked in on a private moment.

"Yes," Cole said.

"No," she uttered at the same time. They were at work. They couldn't admit to having private moments. "It's fine. What can I do for you?"

Braden looked from her to Cole, his expression suspicious. "I wanted to discuss the players and schedule for the weekend. Since we didn't have time to talk about them at dinner the other night."

Oh, he did not just do that, she thought, narrowing her gaze.

"I realize we had *other* things to discuss. Private things," Braden continued, clearly determined to make a point in front of the other man.

She stiffened at his insinuation that there had been

something personal between them.

"What's going on? Do you two know each other outside of work?" Cole asked.

"We do," she said, keeping things deliberately vague, and her pointed stare warned Braden to keep his mouth shut about their past.

He treated her to a curt nod.

"Why didn't you say something sooner?" Cole sounded as hurt as he was confused.

Guilt filled her. "It's complicated and I'll explain everything when I get back, okay? In the meantime, Dr. Prescott and I need to talk."

Taking a step back, Cole looked between them, giving her a chance to contrast the two men.

There were obvious differences, the hair and eye color, the fact that Cole was lean with more of a golfer's build whereas Braden was built more like his brother Damon and worked out, giving him a more muscled appearance. Personality wise, they couldn't be more opposite, either. Cole was more of a relaxed, beta type, where Braden opted for a take-charge attitude.

One guess which she was more attracted to. She sighed and faced Cole.

"If I don't see you before you go, have a good trip," he said.

"Thank you," she said. "I'll touch base when I get

back." Or more likely she'd see him at work first.

One last glance at them both and Cole strode out. She could only imagine the conclusions he'd drawn.

Furious, she braced her hands on her hips and turned to Braden. "What was that about? Peeing on your territory, which I am not?"

"Babe, he ran out with his tail between his legs. He's not the guy for you."

She held back a growl of frustration, refusing to admit Braden had a point. "What did you want?"

He sat down on the edge of her desk, looking comfortable and at ease. "I wanted to say hello and see if you were ready to go. Which I see from your bag that you are."

"What happened to discussing players and the weekend schedule?" She tapped her foot against the floor, already knowing it had been an excuse to interrupt them.

"I just wanted to come by and say hi." He shrugged. "Don't blame me if Mr. Nice Guy let himself be run off. How are you?"

"I'm fine. Looking forward to your first away game?" she asked.

"Hoping you'll show me the ropes. Are these away weekends really jam-packed?"

She nodded. "We'll touch down, get to the hotel, and the players and coaches will go into meetings.

There's a dinner and curfew. Then we'll be at the stadium bright and early, taking care of business, and fly home that same night."

His phone buzzed and he glanced at the text. "I'm being summoned. See you on the bus and, if not, on the plane," he said because they took multiple buses to the airport.

She nodded and walked over to her desk, sitting down in her chair.

"Willow?"

She jerked her head up, surprised to see he hadn't yet left.

"Save me a seat on the plane," he said with a wink.

And then he was gone.

"Argh." She laid her head down on the desk and groaned.

The man was a tease and he tested her restraint. But at least she knew, with well over one hundred people traveling with the team, she wouldn't have to spend time with him except when their paths crossed on the field or during conversation over certain players.

She'd have no problem keeping him at a distance.

*   *   *

THE TRIP TO Denver was long, and the team rented its own huge plane. Braden boarded late, having been held up by a quick meeting with the other doctors traveling with him. He wasn't surprised to see that Willow had chosen an aisle seat next to one of her trainers, leaving no room for him to join her.

He stifled a grin. She really was making him work for the smallest inroads, and he sobered at the reason why. During their time together, she'd given him a small grasp on her history. She never liked to talk about her childhood. He just knew she'd grown up in foster care and not with a big family like he'd had around him.

For all that Jesse Prescott had been a difficult father, Braden had had his mother, his four siblings, and his *uncle* Paul and his partner, Ron. He and his siblings had only recently discovered that Paul was their biological father via sperm donation. Another story for another time, he thought, wryly. But their lives would have been much different had Paul raised them instead.

Either way, though, Braden had had love and he'd had people he could count on. Willow had had no one. At least not until Dr. Jonas and his wife took her in, but by then the emotional damage had been done. She expected people to leave and kept them at a distance in anticipation. He'd played right into her expectations.

He was ready to work for his redemption.

When they arrived at the hotel, room keys were

handed out. Rookies shared a room. Veteran players had their own rooms. As it turned out, he was solo, which he appreciated. Since leaving Brazil, he'd gotten used to the peace and quiet of being on his own and not sharing a tent.

As he entered the elevator and pulled his suitcase to the back, other people piled in, the last being Willow.

He didn't think she noticed him.

"Can you press fifteen?" she asked someone standing closer to the panel, facing forward.

Braden glanced at the paper key holder with his room number written on it and grinned. The elevator stopped on various floors, and people pushed their way out until the car finally paused on fifteen. Since she was at the front, Willow walked out without looking behind her.

He excused himself, and someone had to step out for Braden to finally exit the elevator car and follow the signs to his room. As he made his way to the end of the hall, he couldn't believe his eyes or his luck.

Willow had just pulled her key from her purse and was inserting the card into the lock in the room next to his. "Hey, neighbor," he said, unable to hide his pleasure.

"You have got to be kidding me. Did you arrange this?" she asked as she pushed open her door, propping it with her suitcase.

"Nope. Just pure luck."

"All of it bad," she muttered, but he didn't take her words all that seriously.

Did she want anything to do with him? Probably not, but he'd been there for their goodbye earlier in the week. He'd heard the hitch in her breath as he'd moved in closer. The trembling of her body as his lips touched her cheek. And when he'd stood up? The pebbling of her nipples visible through her shirt.

If it were just sexual desire he had to worry about, he could break through her walls, but he wanted more. And for that he needed to prove to her he was a man she could rely on. One who wouldn't abandon her again.

He opened his own door and immediately caught sight of the connecting door to her room.

Things just kept getting better and better.

* * *

OF ALL THE rooms in this massive hotel, how had Braden ended up adjoining hers? Willow glanced at the closed door that not only separated her and Braden but mocked her because it would be so easy to unlock it and knock on his side. Nope. She wasn't doing it. This was a business weekend, and that's how she would treat it.

After unpacking, she headed downstairs for dinner, sitting at a table with her fellow trainers and physical therapists who'd come on the trip. She was aware of Braden nearby with the doctors and some staff from the front office, but she did her best to focus on the conversation around her and contribute where she could.

After dinner, she retreated to her room, determined to get a good night's sleep in preparation for an early game day tomorrow. She showered and changed into a pair of pajama shorts and a tank top, pulling her hair into a damp bun on top of her head. To be sure she woke up on time, she set up her phone's alarm for repeat after the first five minutes and plugged in the charging cord.

She was about to climb into bed when a dull knock sounded, and it wasn't coming from the door to the hallway, either. She waited, and the sound came again from the room next door, and her stomach did a flip.

She walked over to the adjoining wall and placed her hand on the door.

"Willow, open up," Braden's deep, masculine voice called out, sounding muffled from the wall between the rooms.

She glanced down at her outfit, decided she was covered enough, drew a deep breath, unlocked and opened the door.

Braden stood waiting, wearing a pair of sweats that rode low on his hips, and there was no denying the bulge in his pants. His chest was bare and tanned, the muscles in his forearms and abs a sight to behold.

She swallowed hard. "Hi."

"Hi. I ordered us dessert." He turned and gestured to the small room-service cart behind him. "Your favorite. Vanilla ice cream brownie sundae. Your room or mine?" he asked.

Her stomach rumbled, completely on board with his gesture. Her emotions were much more wary, but she wasn't about to let the dessert melt. "Come on in." She swept her arm toward her room.

With her help, they maneuvered the cart into the small room and settled it in front of the double beds so they could sit down and eat. There wasn't enough room to pull up two chairs, and they wound up side by side on the edge of one bed.

"You really didn't need to do this," she said as she picked up a spoon.

He shrugged. "I wanted to. Besides, I figured you wouldn't slam the door in my face if I came bearing food."

He knew her too well. "You're right. This looks delicious. Thank you."

"Can we consider it a peace offering?" He met her gaze, sincerity and a genuine need to make things right in his expression, and she sighed.

She certainly couldn't go on with an angry wall between them. He'd lived his life as he chose, and she couldn't hold that against him any longer.

"Peace," she murmured in agreement.

He held her stare, his answering smile full of warmth in a way that spoke to her soul.

It unnerved her, and unable to look into his eyes any longer, she focused on the ice cream, taking a spoonful, making sure to get the brownie on it, too. She put the treat into her mouth and moaned at the mixture of chocolate, cold vanilla flavor.

"What did I tell you about that sound?" he asked, his voice a low growl.

Her stomach flipped at the distinct memory. *Do not make that sound around me unless you're prepared for what happens next.*

The following moments were sexually charged, her body suddenly tingling with awareness with his gaze still hot on hers. Mesmerized by the intensity sizzling between them, she couldn't break eye contact, memories of the past colliding in her mind. His hands cupping her face, his mouth devouring hers, their bodies meshing perfectly in bed. A hot flush rose to her cheeks, and she felt the puckering of her nipples beneath her flimsy tank top.

Watching her, he cupped the back of her head. She

didn't pull away, so he urged her to lean forward, his breath warm and oh so close. A voice in the back of her head asked her what in the world she was doing, but she couldn't stop what was happening between them.

And when his mouth touched hers, all thoughts, good and bad, fled completely. His tongue slid across her lips and she moaned. He stiffened at the sound and then began to kiss her in earnest, their tongues tangling as he tasted her, devoured her. He kissed like a dream, even better than in her memories, and she melted into him, wanting more, and he seemed all too willing to give her what she needed.

He tipped her head to the side, giving himself deeper access, and he swept his tongue throughout her mouth. They stayed that way for a long while, making out like two people who'd been apart for a long time. And that was the thought that brought her back to her senses. They *had* been separated because he'd easily walked away.

Who was to say he wouldn't do it again?

She was about to pull back when he did it first, but not before sweeping his tongue over her lips once more.

"You taste like the sweetest dessert," he said, running a hand through her hair.

He tasted so delicious she wanted to dive in for

more. But her heart reminded her of all the reasons she shouldn't. "Mind if I finish the ice cream before it melts?"

"Go for it." He released her, and she felt his stare as she took another bite of the brownie, the vanilla already melting over the warm chocolate.

"You didn't get yourself one?"

He shook his head. "Still full from dinner."

She nodded. "So what are your plans beyond working for the team? I know most of the doctors have practices they're at when they aren't needed at the stadium."

Leaning back on one hand, he said, "Hudson and I found a health center downtown that's in need of doctors. We're going to stop by this week and see if we can donate our time now and add more hours when the season is over."

Interesting, she thought. "So you liked the humanitarian aspect of the work you did for MSF?" She tilted her head, truly curious about how he'd changed since his time away.

He nodded. "I want to help people who need it, and I can do that here, too."

She admired his dedication to helping others. He'd done charitable work all through his med school years, and it had ultimately led him to Doctors Without Borders. He was a good, compassionate man, and knowing that made it even harder to remain angry. The hurt still remained, duller now but no less present.

"Do you miss being away?" she asked.

He immediately shook his head. "No. I'm happy to be back with my family." He paused, waiting for her to meet his gaze before continuing. "And with you."

She slid her tongue over her lips and put the spoon down on the makeshift table. "I think we should call it a night. We have to be up early." Things had gotten carried away and deep enough for one night. At least for her.

He took the hint and stood. "Let's pull this outside," he said of the room-service cart.

She opened the hall door for him, and he eased the cart outside before returning.

"About the kiss…" she began.

He leaned against the entry leading to his room, looking extremely sexy as his intent gaze met hers. "You're going to say it shouldn't have happened, but I disagree. And I'm sure when you're lying in bed tonight thinking of my mouth on yours, you'll feel differently. Even if it kills you to admit it."

He leaned in and briefly touched his lips to hers before walking into his room and closing the door behind him.

And as she shut her side of the connecting doors, her lips weren't the only part of her body tingling.

*   *   *

BRADEN SAT DOWN on his bed and groaned, adjusting his cock behind his sweats. Walking out of Willow's room hadn't been easy, but it had definitely been the right thing to do. Though he'd allowed himself to get lost in the kiss, he'd remained attuned to her feelings every step of the way and sensed the minute she mentally and emotionally disconnected. Her body had stiffened, and before she could stop kissing him, he'd broken contact and backed away first.

She didn't trust him, and to push harder or to sleep with her would only lead to her having regrets. He wanted to build something solid, not have things break down even further. So here he was, alone in his hotel room, with the woman he wanted on the other side of the wall.

Besides, she might not be in a serious relationship with another man, but there was something between Willow and Cole, and it needed to end before they progressed sexually. She wasn't the type of woman to cheat on a man, and he had a feeling once the adrenaline from their kiss wore off, she wouldn't be happy with herself. Braden could only hope that kiss showed her what was missing in her life and push her to end things with Cole.

The night passed, and before he knew it, they were on the field for the game the next day. They worked as a team through injuries—one concussion, a high ankle sprain, and myriad of other issues—and after a win, they were back on the plane and headed home.

No sooner had he walked into his apartment than his phone rang. He glanced down to see his mother calling. Christine Prescott was a good parent who'd done her best despite a challenging marriage to a tough man, and Braden didn't hold his father's behavior against her. She knew his schedule so he wasn't concerned about her calling so late.

He hit reply. "Hey, Mom," he said as he locked up and headed straight to his bedroom.

"Welcome home."

He chuckled. "Do you have radar? I just got here." He dropped his bag on the floor of his bedroom, leaving the unpacking for another time.

"I figured as much. Did you have a good trip?" she asked.

"It's a whirlwind," he said of his time in Denver. "I can't believe they play, turn around, and return on the same night only to practice again first thing Monday morning. It's crazy."

"You sound like it was fun, though."

He grinned, thinking of the rush of standing on the field, sprinting to someone's aid, watching Willow tape up an injury and send the player back out to play. "It was exhilarating."

"I must say I'm relieved to hear that," she mur-mured.

"Relieved? Why?" He kicked off his shoes and stretched out on the bed.

"Because it means you're really home to stay. Your family is here and you belong with us. And speaking of family, I wanted to talk to you about Thanksgiving."

He blinked up at the ceiling. "Wow. I hadn't thought about the holiday. It's in what? Two weeks?"

"Exactly," his mom said. "Now the Thunder isn't playing on Thursday, and Damon's lucky enough to be in the same city as his family. He's bringing some of the players home with him. We're going to be a huge crowd this year. So feel free to bring anyone you want."

He grinned at his mom's generous heart. "Hudson will be there for sure." His best friend's family was on the East Coast, and given that he was avoiding going home, Braden assumed Hudson would rather remain in Miami and work.

"He's more than welcome, but I was thinking of a certain blonde I saw standing beside you on the sidelines."

He let out a groan. His mom had always liked Wil-low, but she wasn't used to big family gatherings, and when they were together, she told him she'd gone to Dr. Jonas's house for holidays.

He couldn't see her wanting to join him this year. "You know we're not together anymore." Which didn't mean he wouldn't invite her.

"Damon might have mentioned he caught you watching her a time or two. Or five," she said on a chuckle.

Braden cursed his brother and his big mouth. The last thing he wanted was to be the subject of family gossip.

"All I'm saying is if you'd like to ask her, she's more than welcome."

He rolled his eyes at her deliberate push. His mother wanted to see all her kids paired off, and she had Braden and Bri left to go. "Thanks, Mom. I'll let you know."

"Okay. Go get some sleep. I love you."

"Love you, too," he said and disconnected the call.

Bracing his hands behind his head, he closed his eyes, knowing he still wanted to jump in the shower before going to sleep.

He just needed a few minutes to unwind. As he closed his eyes, his mind drifted to Willow, and he grabbed his phone, deciding to text her. He wanted to be the last thing she thought of before falling asleep.

Chapter Four

*T*HINKING OF YOU. *Hope you dream about me.* A full-body tremor rippled through Willow every time she recalled Braden's bedtime text.

His words stayed with her all through the day as she worked on her patients, their bodies battered and bruised from yesterday's game. To her utter mortification, it wasn't until she saw Cole the next day that she realized what she'd done.

Kissing Braden and falling into that zone of pleasure had wiped out all thoughts of anyone else. Including the man she was casually dating. If she could make out with Braden with no consideration for Cole, if Braden could take her outside herself so easily, Cole Walsh wasn't the man for her. Something she'd been avoiding completely admitting to herself, and now she had to do something about it.

But today kept her too busy to think about her personal life. She iced, taped, used stim, and more throughout the day, and by the time she could leave, she was exhausted and Cole was gone for the night. Instead of heading straight home, she'd promised Bella

Jonas she'd stop by after work, and she didn't want to disappoint her.

She pulled up to the house where she'd spent the end of her teenage years and parked in the driveway. With Peter in jail and unable to post bail because Bella had refused to put up the house as collateral, Bella was here alone.

Willow shut the engine, grabbed her purse, and exited the car. She headed up the path leading to the front door and rang the doorbell, but Bella must have heard or seen her approach, because she opened the door at the same time.

"Hi! I'm so glad you're here!" Bella, a petite brunette wearing a pair of jeans and a light sweater, greeted Willow with a smile.

"Hi, yourself!"

They hugged before Bella shut the door, and they walked to the kitchen, where they always ended up sitting to chat.

"I put aside dinner for you. Let me heat it in the microwave." Bella rushed around the kitchen, bringing back warm memories of her making dinner when Willow lived there.

She remembered being in awe of someone who was always happy and wary of her kindness. With time and patience, Bella had won Willow over. It was impossible not to love the woman who had taken in many foster kids over the years because she couldn't have children of her own.

"How are you, really?" Willow asked. She didn't need to elaborate. Bella would understand what Willow was referring to.

She sighed heavily. "I'm managing. I'm not taking Peter's calls and I'm having divorce papers drawn up."

Willow was surprised. "It hasn't been that long since the news broke. Are you sure you don't want to take time to think about it some more?" she asked as the microwave beeped, indicating the food was finished heating. "You were married a long time."

Bella retrieved the plate and put it down in front of Willow at the kitchen table. Bella had already set the table and given Willow a glass of ice water. The delicious smell of Bella's signature chicken potpie wafted up, and Willow took a bite, the creamy flavor so good.

Bella settled into a chair across from Willow. "No matter how I look at the situation, he lied about so many things. His gambling addiction, the money he owed, the taxes he didn't pay." She shook her head. "If he'd told me he had a problem, I could have gotten him help. He betrayed everything about our marriage and our relationship. And what he did to Damon Prescott? Taking money to inject him with perfor-mance-enhancing drugs? I don't know that man and I don't want to."

From her tone of voice, Bella meant her words, and Willow didn't blame her and she sighed. "I understand. I'm just sad for you."

"I'll be okay. Now you eat."

With a smile at Bella's insistence, Willow finished her meal, realizing as she ate just how hungry she was. Once full, she gathered her plate and utensils and walked to the sink and, over Bella's objections, began rinsing and cleaning up.

"So I watched the game yesterday," Bella said as Willow finished and wiped her hands on a dishtowel.

Willow wasn't surprised Bella had viewed the game without her husband being around. They were a football family through and through and had instilled that love of the game in Willow.

Rejoining Bella at the table, she said, "It was a good game. A win."

Bella smiled. "I also saw the press conference introducing the new doctor streamed on the team's website. Very interesting choice. Don't you think?"

Willow's gaze shot to Bella's. "Don't go there." She didn't want to think about Braden and the things he made her feel.

"You're defensive, which is exactly why we *should* go there. How has it been working with him?" Bella stared at Willow until she squirmed in her seat.

She twisted her hands together and forced a smile. "It's been okay. No problem."

"R-i-g-h-t. That's why you're wringing your hands together. Your nerves are so completely obvious."

Willow unclasped her fingers that now ached. "I'm serious. It's been fine. If you count getting stuck with adjoining rooms in Denver fine."

Bella's green eyes opened wide. "What?"

Though Willow hadn't planned to discuss kissing Braden with anyone, she sat with the closest thing to a mother she'd ever had and knew she needed someone to listen.

She cleared her throat. "So the rooms were a fluke. But Saturday night he knocked and brought in a room-service cart with my favorite dessert."

Bella's gaze softened. "That was nice."

"It's easy to offer up a sweet gesture. It won't make me forget how easily he left."

She tipped her head to the side. "Oh, sweetie." She grasped Willow's hand and squeezed tight. "You have abandonment issues and rightly so. We don't have to get into the whys or what happened to you. Not now. But I hope one day we can dig into things, because you need to get the pain out. Was Braden wrong? Absolutely. But what does he say now?"

"Before or after we kissed?" Willow asked.

Bella leaned on the table, her eyes opened wide,

her surprised expression speaking for itself.

"Umm, yes. He says he wishes he'd handled things differently. But that doesn't matter. The very fact that he did it means I can't trust him to stick around." And she didn't plan on giving him the opportunity to repeat the past.

"Hmm. Now for an even harder question. What about Cole?"

Willow sighed. "I need to end things with him. It's the right thing to do."

"And Braden?"

She shook her head. "I can't let myself go there."

"Something tells me Braden doesn't agree." Patting Willow's hand, she offered her a smile. "Good luck talking to Cole and dealing with Braden."

"Thanks." Willow rose from her seat. "I should get going. I have to be up early, as usual."

Bella stood and walked with Willow to the door. "Oh! I'm going to my sister's this year for Thanksgiving, and you're more than welcome to join me and I hope you will. Kathy would love to see you."

Willow forced a smile. She didn't know how she felt about being with another big family for the holiday. She was used to a small gathering with Bella and Peter or being alone. "I'll let you know. Thank you and thank Kathy for the invitation." Leaning over, she kissed Bella's cheek. "I loved catching up."

"Same here. I'll talk to you soon."

She walked out to her car, climbed inside, and headed home, needing a good night's sleep, because from Cole to Braden, tomorrow would definitely be a difficult day.

* * *

BRADEN FOLLOWED THE directions to the health center, making a series of right and left turns that took him deeper into the center of the city, Hudson in the passenger seat. They left the luxury area of South Beach and headed downtown, the scenery changing. More dilapidated buildings, more depressed neighborhoods, more people in need of good medical care. He pulled his SUV into the parking lot and cut the engine.

"I'm glad we finally have a chance to check things out here," Hudson said, stretching his legs out in front of him at the same time moving his seat back for comfort, a little late considering they'd been in the car for twenty minutes.

"Tuesday is game planning. It's the only free time we do have. Cole and Marshall can handle any injury issues that come up today." As the sun hit the windshield at an awkward angle, Braden adjusted his sunglasses and put the visor down.

"How's it going with Willow?"

"Avoidance at its finest," he muttered. "She's a

tough nut to crack. Not that I blame her. She's a child of foster care. Moved around a lot. She puts up walls to keep from getting hurt. She let me in and I blew things. It's going to take more than an I'm sorry to make her believe in me again." It was the first time he'd spoken about Willow's past and her issues. As much as he respected her privacy, he needed an ear and some advice. "So the question is, do I push or give her space?"

"I say push. What's space going to get you but more of the same? Being ignored." Hudson shrugged and glanced out the window.

"Good point." Braden cut the engine and they exited the car, meeting up in the graveled lot.

"The outside leaves a lot to be desired," Braden said, checking out the building you couldn't even tell was a health clinic but for the small sign in the window.

"I hope the equipment inside is up-to-date and working. Not to mention the state of their supplies." Hudson strode up to the glass and peered inside. "Hard to tell."

Braden opened the door, and they walked into a full waiting room with what was clearly a barely working air conditioning unit. He stopped at the check-in window.

A woman glanced up at him, looking harried.

"How can I help you? Though I should warn you it's a long wait. We're short-staffed."

He leaned an arm on the counter. "Actually that's why we're here. We're doctors interested in joining the staff. Can we speak to whoever's in charge?"

"Dr. Anderson!" the woman spun around and called out toward the back of the area. "Two doctors here to see you! You're going to want to talk to them."

Turning, Braden raised an eyebrow at Hudson, who shrugged.

Half an hour later, they'd been given a tour of the facility, such as it was, three exam rooms in the back, a storage area that needed organization, an X-ray machine that lacked a technician, and a donated ultrasound machine. Basically, they were making do with the bare minimum and that included doctors on hand and ready to help.

Dr. Thomas Anderson had welcomed them without question. The clinic operated on a sliding scale of what a patient could afford and, according to Tom, as he liked to be called, was hanging on by a thread. Braden and Hudson were badly needed.

Braden knew he'd have the time. Ian had assured him once he had his footing with the players, he could fall into a routine with overseeing the athletes here, and like the other doctors, he could either work at a medical practice or, as he wanted to do, this healthcare clinic.

As they were talking, the receptionist began to call out. "One man with chest pains, another with severe bleeding, and a pregnant woman with cramping!"

Tom looked from Braden to Hudson, who shrugged. "I've got the bleeder."

"I'll take the chest pains," Tom said.

"Send me the pregnant patient." Braden headed to the nearest sink to scrub his hands. He wasn't an obstetrician, but he'd delivered babies with much less equipment in much less sterile conditions, so he felt sure he could handle this situation.

The young woman, a blonde named Aurora Michaels, said she was eighteen and seven months pregnant. She'd been into the center earlier in her pregnancy and hadn't been back since. She just barely met the metrics for a safe weight at this stage of her pregnancy, and she appeared exhausted, causing his heart to twist at the sight.

He examined her, then used the sonogram machine to check on the baby, making conversation as he ran the wand over her stomach. "Are the contractions regular?" he asked.

"No. They just made me nervous. It's too early to have my baby," she said, tears in her eyes along with the trembling fear in her voice.

"Well, that's a good sign. Are the contractions getting stronger?"

She shook her head. "It's just a tightening that's uncomfortable and it comes and goes."

"Okay, let's see. Do you want to know if you're having a boy or a girl?"

Her eyes opened wide. "I… Yes. Please."

He didn't have to look too intently. "It's a girl," he said with a smile. "And she looks good."

The young woman on the table visibly relaxed, a tear slipping out of one eye. Poor kid, he thought, wondering if she was all alone. He'd have to tiptoe carefully in order to find out.

"Are you getting enough sleep? I know it's harder the later you go in the third trimester." He'd start with basic questions about her life and hope for truthful answers.

She bit down on her lip. "Sometimes. Depends on the night."

"And food? Are you eating okay?" he asked, checking measurements of the baby's head. All looked good. He breathed out his own sigh of relief.

She nodded. "The diner where I work lets me eat for free."

"Yeah? Is the food good?"

She treated him to a small smile. "Not bad. Merry's husband, Sonny, is a pretty good cook."

"What's the name? Maybe I'll check it out sometime."

"Merry's," she said.

"After Merry. Got it." He tucked the information away and decided to push a little further. "What about your living arrangements?"

This time she pulled her lip into her mouth before letting go. "I'm fine."

He cleaned off the transducer and hooked it onto the side of the machine, covering her belly with a sheet before meeting her gaze. "Just tell me you're not living on the street, because if you are, I can help you find a safe place to stay."

She shook her head. "There's a back room in the diner. Merry and Sonny let me stay there. They've been good to me."

"I'm glad." He wondered about the baby's father but decided to let it go for now. "Any family?" he couldn't not ask. As much as it was his job to treat the patient, he had a driving need to be sure she was safe, as well.

She shook her head. "I aged out of foster care. I was already pregnant at the time. But I get by," she said defensively, her foster care story reminding him of a different blonde he knew and whose walls he was also trying to breach.

"I'm sure you are. Do you have a plan for post-delivery?" She couldn't continue to stay in the back room of a diner with a baby.

"Am I finished? You said the baby's okay, right? So what's with the contractions?"

She put a barrier up between them, and he took her words as a no. No plan for herself and her child once she was born. Since he'd be working here, he hoped he could see her more often and help her figure out what she was going to do. For now, he'd pried enough.

He rose from his stool. "You're not in preterm labor, which is good news. What you're experiencing are called Braxton Hicks contractions. It's the body's way of getting ready for delivery," he assured her. "But you did the right thing coming here."

She released another heavy breath. "Okay, good."

"You can get dressed now. I think you should come back once a week." At this stage and with a normal pregnancy, an obstetrician would see a patient every two weeks, but with her precarious living and support situation, he'd feel better keeping an eye on her.

Her hand came to her stomach. "But I don't have insurance."

"We'll work things out. Just make an appointment and come back. Please."

She eyed him warily and didn't answer, so he started for the door. "Nice to meet you, Aurora." He smiled warmly and hoped he'd see her in this clinic again next week.

They rolled up their sleeves, so to speak, and stayed for the day, during which Braden learned how much they were needed here. He left feeling more productive than he had since leaving MSF.

Back at their apartment building, he and Hudson parted ways, Braden making his way upstairs to his unit. He tossed his keys onto the counter and pulled his phone from his pocket, checking his messages. His sister wanted to meet for a catch-up lunch, and his mother had checked in.

But the one person he wanted to hear from remained stubbornly silent.

*   *   *

THE PLAYERS HAD all gone home for the night, and Willow took the time to type notes onto the computer about the patients she'd treated, long-term plans, and her thoughts on their ability to play. After finishing up, she sent the file to both the head orthopedist and Braden for the upcoming week's game. She knew Cole was staying late, as well, so as soon as she finished work and shut down for the night, she drew a deep breath and headed to find him.

She discovered him in an office he shared with the other team doctors, but he was alone.

"Hey there," she said, announcing her presence so she didn't startle him.

"Hi!" He turned from his computer, a smile spread across his face.

He was obviously happy to see her, but that wouldn't be the case in a few minutes, once she said what she had to say.

"I was just finishing up for the night." He rose to his feet and came around the desk. "I didn't expect to see you." He reached for her hands, but she kept hers at her sides.

"I've been … busy," she murmured.

"Busy avoiding me?" He nailed her behavior completely and she sighed.

There was no doubt Cole was a handsome man, and maybe, given time, she could have developed feelings for him, but she'd never feel that explosive desire for him that Braden elicited inside her. And after seeing Braden again, experiencing that out-of-this-world kiss, she knew she wanted much more than companionship with any man she chose.

Cole deserved more than a woman who couldn't give him her heart. "Not avoiding you exactly," she hedged. "But I do need to talk to you."

His expression fell, the smile gone. "I had a feeling. Care to tell me why? I thought we enjoyed each other's company."

How did she explain? Mentioning Braden was out of the question for so many reasons, her professionalism being paramount. "Can we say it's not you, it's me?" she asked, cringing as she used those trite words.

"I'm not sure it matters why, but can I ask if it's about Braden Prescott?"

She blinked in surprise. "What makes you say that?"

"Which isn't a no." He shoved his hands into his chinos pockets. "I saw you two on the sidelines last week and briefly on television this past weekend. There's a certain chemistry between you that's hard to miss."

She swallowed over the lump in her throat and realized she had to tell him the truth. "We're not together now but we have history," she admitted.

"It's obvious. And you should have told me," he said, sounding hurt.

She stepped forward to put a hand on his shoulder, then thought better of it. "Probably but I wanted to keep the past in the past and my private life private."

"Not so easy when you're working with your ex. He *is* your ex, right? That's what you mean by history?"

She nodded.

"Well, I see something current brewing between you two now." He met her gaze, his expression cool.

"You should be careful. I heard him telling stories about his time traveling for Doctors Without Borders, and the man definitely lit up when he talked about his time there. Who knows how long he'll stick around."

Although Willow didn't know if he was looking out for her or trying to hurt her, she was annoyed just the same. As for Braden, Cole wasn't telling her anything she didn't already know. But it still hurt to hear and reminded her of why she needed to keep her emotional walls high.

"I don't appreciate you making assumptions about me or gossiping about my life." Braden joined them, a pissed-off expression on his face, arms folded across his chest.

Cole glanced at Braden and, without another word, shook his head and walked out of his own office, leaving them alone. Her stomach twisted at the way things had ended. She'd wanted an easier breakup, but he'd taken her off guard. The fact that both Bella and Cole had picked up on something between her and Braden meant others would, too. And she didn't like it at all.

"So what was that all about?" Braden asked.

"It's really none of your business." She did not want to tell him she'd ended things with Cole and have him make all sorts of assumptions as to why.

There was no reason for him to know his kiss had

been the impetus for her to take that step because she wasn't the kind of woman to lead a man on.

Braden narrowed his gaze. "Considering he mentioned me by name and had the balls to come to pretty wrong conclusions about my life, I'd say it's very much my business."

She leaned against the desk, gripping the edge with her hands. "We broke up," she said through clenched teeth.

Interest flashed in his gorgeous eyes. "I take it from how pissed off he was that you're the one who ended things?"

He stepped into her personal space, and when she drew a breath, it was his cologne she smelled, his sexy frame that was close to hers, and as usual, her own body responded.

"Does it matter?" she asked.

"It does to me. I want to know that our kiss meant something to you. Enough to break up with Walsh." He leaned in and she stopped him, placing her hand on his chest.

Eyes leveled on hers, he grasped her wrist and pulled her toward him, placing her palm against his mouth. She shivered, the soft feel of his lips a whisper she felt everywhere. Her nipples tightened and her sex clenched, moisture coating her silk underwear. She held back a moan, but she knew there was no missing the evidence of her arousal, not when his gaze zeroed in on her chest.

"Admit it. I'm the reason you ended things," he said in a raspy tone. He threaded his fingers through hers.

"Even if you were, it doesn't change things between us." But the pulsing desire flowing through her begged her to change her mind.

"You just cleared the way, sweetheart. I'm a Prescott and a Dare. We know how to get what we want." His gaze bored into hers, making it abundantly clear exactly what he meant.

She decided not to dignify his comment with a reply, but clearly he wasn't put off, because he merely grinned at her. "So what are you doing for Thanksgiving this year?" he asked.

She took the subject change as a good sign. "I'm not sure. Bella may go to her sister's and she invited me, but she lives a couple of hours away…" She trailed off and shrugged. "I'm not sure. I think I'd rather stay close and do my own thing."

"In other words, spend the holiday alone?" His frown told her what he thought of that idea.

"I'm used to it. Now if you'll excuse me, it's been a long day and I'm tired. I'd like to go home."

He nodded. "I'll walk you to your car."

She opened her mouth to argue and he shook his

head.

Fine, he could escort her out. She hoped this wasn't the beginning of having him around her constantly, because despite the warnings that came with Braden Prescott, he was extremely hard to resist.

Chapter Five

IF WILLOW THOUGHT Braden would let her spend Thanksgiving alone, she had another thing coming. Despite her intention to hole up in her apartment, he had a plan. One he wouldn't tell her ahead of time or she'd find a way to avoid being home when he rang her doorbell.

In the two weeks leading up to the holiday, he made sure to work closely with her when he could, bring lunch to her, join her in her office to eat and make small talk, and just get to know her again.

In between, he worked at the health center, getting to know the regulars and meeting the patients as they came in for either emergency or regular medical care. To his dismay, Aurora didn't show up again, which both upset him and had him worrying about her and her baby. He hadn't had a chance to check out where she worked and the place she called home, but it was on his agenda for tomorrow morning before he went to his mom's for holiday dinner.

That night, he and Hudson walked to their cars. They had one day off tomorrow before game weekend prep began. Most players would come in the morning to train and exercise, regardless of the holiday, which meant some physicians and trainers would be on duty, but he and Hudson were off. So, he knew, was Willow. He'd made it his business to check schedules.

"What time should I come to your house tomorrow?" Hudson asked as they strode through the facility.

"I'm going to the clinic before I head over for dinner. I hope to get there around four," he said. "I think the rest of the family will show up any time from two o'clock on. Mom has food out all day. So basically it's up to you."

"Did you ask Willow what she's doing for the holiday?" Hudson pulled open the door leading to the parking lot, and they stepped outside into the warm air.

Braden nodded. "I did. She said she's going to be home alone, and I plan on changing up her plans. I just haven't mentioned it to her."

Hudson chuckled. "I don't know if you're brave or stupid."

"Probably a little of both but what's that expression? No pain no gain? She needs some prodding out of her safe little world. There's no other way I can prove she can trust me again."

He didn't just intend to bring her to his mom's

house for dinner and not take no for an answer but he had a way to convince that she couldn't turn down.

He glanced at his friend. "What about you? Anyone you want to bring over for dinner? I know Mom wouldn't mind."

"No, thanks. You have enough siblings for me to hang out with. So you're bringing Willow. Is Bri coming with a date?" Hudson asked as they reached their cars, parked near each other.

"Not that I know of." He hit the button on his key fob and his car locks opened. "Why?"

Hudson shrugged. "You're all paired off. Just wondered if I was going to be lone man there."

"As far as I know, Bri's single. Though she keeps her dating life pretty private. At least from her brothers."

Hudson grinned. "Can't say I blame her on that score. Okay, I'll see you tomorrow."

"See you." Braden climbed into his car and started the engine, planning his day tomorrow carefully in his mind.

He had two women on his mind. One needed him professionally, the other he needed personally, but the irony was he thought Willow could help with Aurora and encourage her to come back to the clinic. They had foster care in common, and maybe Willow could use her past to bond with the pregnant woman and encourage her to trust Braden.

Not to mention it gave him an excuse to visit her on Thanksgiving Day, to get her to spend the morning with him, talking to a patient, and end up at his mom's house for holiday dinner. Willow might be able to resist him, but she wouldn't be able to turn her back on someone in need. The fact that he benefitted from the entire scenario was a bonus. One he planned to use shamelessly to his advantage.

*   *   *

WILLOW HAD DEBATED all week on whether or not she wanted to cook a holiday dinner for herself and ultimately went with a small turkey breast and a baked sweet potato. Simple and easy. She took out the meat the night before and, once it was defrosted, seasoned it and put it aside for later. It didn't bother her that she was alone. She was used to it, more or less. Although she spent some holidays with Bella and Peter, there were others when they'd visited family and she'd been by herself.

Of course, she would prefer to find someone to share her life with, but she'd tried that with Braden, and not only had he left her, when she looked back, she realized she hadn't been that good at being part of a couple. She held a lot of herself back out of fear of being abandoned. It had been one of the reasons she hadn't gone to Braden's family for any of the celebratory holidays.

The times she'd been with them, each sibling had been more than nice to her, but she'd always felt like she was on the outside looking in at a loving family. In the end, nothing Braden ended up doing had convinced her that her self-protective behavior had been a mistake. She could only imagine how much worse his leaving would have been if she'd let him in all the way.

Settling onto the sofa, she turned on the television and changed the channel so she could watch the parade. Later she'd view the football game while she cooked dinner. She didn't often get a chance to kick back and relax, and today she planned to do just that.

No sooner had she put her bare feet up on the couch than the doorbell rang. She stood up and walked to the peephole, shocked to see Braden on the other side.

As usual, her body responded, her stomach doing an excited flip. She drew a deep breath and prepared herself for an argument about her spending Thanksgiving alone versus with him and his family.

She opened the door and greeted him with a smile. "Well, this is a surprise."

"A good one, I hope."

"That depends on why you're here. Come on in." She stepped aside, and he brushed past her, the scent of his cologne potent and alluring.

She'd already taken in how sexy he looked in jeans that molded to his thighs and the hint of a bulge in the front of his pants. God, the man was everything hot wrapped in the perfect package.

Shutting the door, she gestured for him to go past the entryway to the living room, where the television was still on.

"Watching the parade?"

"Mmm-hmm. I love the floats." She cleared her throat. "So what brings you by?"

He turned away from the TV. "I've been working at a health care center downtown. I think I mentioned it to you?"

She nodded.

"There's a young girl who came in. Name's Aurora. She's eighteen, pregnant, and all alone. She lives in a room behind the diner where she works. She eats for free there, and the owners are good to her, but from looking at her, it's obvious she's underweight and scared."

She blinked in surprise, the subject taking her off guard. She would have sworn he'd come to invite her to dinner. Now that he hadn't, she didn't know if she was disappointed or relieved. And what did that say about her fluctuating feelings for this man that she couldn't decide?

"I'm really sorry. Where is her family?"

Braden's gaze met hers. "She aged out of foster care and found out she was pregnant. Other than the diner owners, she really has no one."

Willow expelled a long breath. It wasn't that long ago she'd aged out herself, but she'd had the Jonases, who hadn't made her leave their home. She could easily imagine herself in the young girl's place, and Willow shivered at the feeling of utter loneliness and fear she must feel.

"Why are you telling me this?" She braced a hand on the wall beside her.

"Because I want to go visit the diner where she works and see if I can't convince her to come to my mom's house for dinner. And I think seeing a woman with me, one who can relate to her on some level, will help her feel safe."

Her heart beat harder at this man's thoughtfulness and caring for his patients. There was no way she could say no. Of course, she knew that he was counting on the childhood she had in common with the girl to encourage Willow to want to help. Which meant she'd have to spend time with Braden, and that was obviously part of his plan. But she couldn't deny how much she felt the need to reach out to the pregnant girl. Being with Braden was a side benefit, as much as it killed her to admit.

"Let me get myself together. I can't exactly go barefoot."

Braden nodded. "Do you have any extra clothes you could bring? I have a feeling Aurora doesn't have much. I know she's pregnant, but she's not huge despite being in her third trimester, and something oversized on top should do."

God, it was hard not to like this man. "Sure," Willow said, a lump in her throat for the girl they were about to go see.

His gaze fell to her feet and a sexy smirk lifted his lips. "Nice toenails."

She glanced down at her Tiffany-blue polish and grinned. "Thank you," she said, pleased with the pedicure she'd given herself, not to mention the fact that he'd noticed, then headed for her bedroom.

A few minutes later, she'd pulled her hair into a messy bun, fixed her face with a little makeup, and put on a swing tank that was nicer than her favorite soft tee shirt with a hole in the bottom. She looked casual and unimposing, which was who she was. Someone a young girl wouldn't find intimidating. Sifting through her clothes, she found a soft, comfy, oversized shirt that was huge on her and a pair of black leggings that maybe the pregnant girl could leave below her belly. Then she slipped on a pair of Chucks and was ready to go.

She met up with him in the living room. "All set. I just need to be home in time to put my turkey in the oven around three." The small breast didn't need more than two to three hours to cook.

He raised an eyebrow. "Do you really think I'm taking Aurora home with me for the holiday and leaving you to eat by yourself? Besides, once Aurora meets you, I bet she's going to be more comfortable with you there."

He had a good point. "You don't play fair," she muttered, knowing arguing would be futile. Although her stomach fluttered with nerves at the prospect of spending hours with his whole family. There were so many siblings and now significant others. She forced in a deep breath and reminded herself she was doing it for a good cause.

He shrugged. "Never said I did." He grasped her elbow and steered her toward the door.

"Wait! I need to put some things in the fridge and grab pie to bring to your mother's."

Obviously certain she wasn't going to hide out in her room, he released his grip and she headed for the kitchen.

"My mom doesn't need pie. She just loves company," he called out.

"I met her once before, remember? I just want to be polite. Besides, why let a good pecan pie go to waste?"

When they were together, he'd wanted her to spend more time with his family. As usual, she'd kept her distance. Maybe that was why he'd had little trouble leaving her. She hadn't given him everything he needed in the relationship or a reason to stay. The thought stunned her. She hadn't considered her own responsibilities in them falling apart.

She bit down on her lower lip, put everything away, and grabbed the pie.

Then they were on their way.

* * *

ONLY WHEN BRADEN had Willow in the passenger seat of his car did he breathe a sigh of relief. She'd joined him without an argument, caring only about Aurora and the situation the young woman found herself in. Willow, despite her hang-ups about getting close to people, had a huge heart. He saw it daily in the way she treated her patients, the players who relied on her talent and ability to get them back on the field.

He'd seen it when they were together the first time and she'd tell him stories about the players she encouraged and helped to believe they would play again after an injury. She was caring and worked overtime to make sure the guys had what they needed. She just didn't know how to accept the same thing for herself that she so easily gave to others.

He'd already put the diner's address into Waze and followed the directions, pulling up in front of Merry's, a restaurant off the beaten path, and parking the car.

The neighborhood wasn't the best, homeless people sitting against buildings and young men congregating in groups wearing similar colors. He knew what that signaled. Aurora wasn't living in a good area, and that concerned him. He didn't know why he felt such a strong need to help this one girl, but he had a hunch it was because she reminded him of who Willow used to be. Not pregnant but a foster care child, too.

She'd been quiet on the way here, and he left her to her thoughts except for the brief conversation on how he wanted to handle their visit.

"We're here," he said, leaning an arm on the steering wheel.

Concern etched her pretty face. She hadn't been expecting him and had only added a little makeup when she'd gone to her bedroom to change. As far as he was concerned, she didn't need it. Fresh face worked for her as much as lightly made up. In fact, he preferred the hint of freckles on her nose.

"Then let's go inside." She exited the vehicle, and he met up with her to walk along the sidewalk, keeping an eye out as they reached the door.

"It's closed," she said, pointing to the sign in the window. She put her hand on her forehead to block out the glare and peeked through the glass.

He frowned and knocked on the door, waited, and knocked again.

"Someone's coming," Willow said.

He heard the rattling of the door being unlocked and suddenly he was face-to-face with Aurora. She wore the same clothes he'd seen her in over two weeks ago, and there were dark circles under her eyes. Clearly she wasn't sleeping well, and waiting tables at the diner wasn't helping. Many pregnant women could work until the end of their pregnancy, but that was if all their other circumstances in life cooperated.

"Dr. Prescott!" Aurora said, obviously surprised to see him. "What are you doing here? I mean, I know you said you'd stop by but it's a holiday. We're closed for business."

"I'm not here to eat. I wanted to check on you."

"Oh." Her fingers curled around the door, her knuckles white.

"Aurora, this is my friend Willow James. We work together at my other job. I'm a team physician for the Miami Thunder. Willow is an athletic trainer."

The young woman's eyes opened wide at that revelation.

"Hi," Willow said with a warm smile.

"Can we come in?" Braden asked. "I'd like to talk to you and see how you're feeling."

Aurora hesitated and then finally nodded, stepping back so they could enter before closing and locking the door behind them. "We can sit at one of the tables." She gestured to a square table with four chairs.

Once they were all sitting, he spoke. "I was hoping you'd come in so I could check you out. How have you been feeling?"

"Better especially since I understand what the cramping pain is." She placed a hand over her belly.

"She was having Braxton Hicks contractions," he said to Willow.

"Aah. I hear they're uncomfortable." Willow rested her elbows on the table, leaned forward, and met Aurora's gaze.

"Yeah." Aurora shook her head. "They're scary, too. I thought I was having real contractions."

They talked for a little while longer about her pregnancy and how she was feeling before Braden said, "If you ladies will excuse me, I'm going to make a quick call."

He shot Willow a pointed glance and headed for the back of the diner, planning to snoop around and see where Aurora was living.

Willow had her own instructions.

*   *   *

WILLOW STUDIED THE young girl who appeared tired and beaten down by life. She bit down on the inside of her cheek and decided to dive in just as Braden had recommended.

"So I take it you're alone here for the holiday?" Willow asked.

Aurora nodded.

"Well, Dr. Prescott and I are going to a family dinner at his mom's house for Thanksgiving. Did you know he has four siblings?"

Aurora shook her head. "He's just a doctor I met once."

"But he's someone who takes an interest in his patients, and he's worried about you. We'd like you to join us for dinner, and before you say no, I want you to know that I'm not all that comfortable going myself. Braden – Dr. Prescott – and I used to date, and it's awkward for me to show up there."

Aurora's eyes had opened wide. "Why does he care if I'm there or not? Why would he invite me?"

"Because he doesn't want you to be alone on a holiday any more than he wanted me to be by myself. He just showed up on my doorstep and announced I was coming with him today." Willow shrugged as if it were normal behavior for him, not wanting to freak the girl out any more than she already was. "Will you come? At least I'll have backup."

Aurora shook her head, her blonde hair swinging across her face. "I can't."

Not won't. Interesting. Leaning forward in her seat, Willow asked, "Why not?"

A long hesitation followed, then Aurora whispered, "I don't have anything to wear." She glanced down at her obviously old shirt and her cheeks flushed with embarrassment.

Willow didn't want to make her feel like a charity case, so she carefully phrased what she said next. "What if I told you I had that covered? I brought an extra shirt that's pretty big and should fit and a pair of leggings?"

Aurora lifted her head and met Willow's gaze, tears in her eyes. "Why would you do that? You don't know me."

Because she so easily could have been in Aurora's shoes, Willow thought. If not for the Jonases she would have aged out and been on her own. But she couldn't tell Aurora she knew about her past without violating the confidence between Braden and his patient.

So she drew a deep breath and decided she had no choice but to tell Aurora her own story. "I grew up in foster care. Between the age of seven and eighteen, I was in five different homes. I didn't have much until my last home, when I was sixteen and was placed with a wonderful family. I know what it's like to be alone, and when Braden told me about you, I just wanted to help."

Aurora sniffed and rubbed her eyes with a napkin on the table. "What happened to your parents? My mom left me with her mom, my grandma, and never came back. Grandma died of breast cancer when I was five. There were no other relatives and I ended up in foster care. I had asthma and was sick a lot. Nobody wanted to adopt a sick kid," Aurora said.

Willow reached across the table and grasped the girl's hand. "I'm sorry about your parents and your grandma."

"Thanks," Aurora said, her gaze on Willow's, waiting for an answer to her question, what happened to her parents?

Willow never talked about her past. Ever. But for this girl, she would. "I have no idea who my father was. My mother said she didn't know. And she … she never picked me up from school one day." She curled her hands into fists in her lap, her nails digging into her skin. "After the police went to check where I lived, they said the apartment had been emptied out." Willow shrugged. "My mother left without a trace."

Aurora wrapped her arms around herself. "I'm sorry, too."

"Now, will you take the clothes and come keep me

company at this big celebration where we'll both feel a little out of place?" She forced a smile past the revelations she'd just made, and to her relief, Aurora grinned back.

"Yeah. I will. Thank you," she said, her tone serious.

"You're welcome." Willow reached into her big purse and pulled out the clothes she'd folded and put inside. "Hopefully they'll fit well enough."

Aurora grabbed the items, a flicker of excitement in her eyes. "I'll go try them on."

Willow turned to watch her go and saw Braden standing behind her. Her face flamed at the realization that he'd heard everything. All the details she'd never told him. That neither her father nor her mother had loved her enough to stick around. She hadn't been enough.

"I didn't want to interrupt." He leaned against one of the pillars in the room, his gaze steady on hers.

She swallowed hard. "So you heard."

He inclined his head. "You never told me any of that," he said in a gruff voice. "And I really wish you had."

"I don't like to talk about my childhood." She rose from her chair, feeling like she needed to be on equal footing with him.

"Yet you just did. For Aurora's sake. That was

sweet and she needs it. I went snooping and saw that back room she's living in." He shook his head. "It barely holds a twin bed. It's more like a closet than a room."

She closed her eyes and sighed, her heart breaking for the young pregnant girl who was barely a woman.

Braden's warm gaze caressed her face, making her tremble, the emotions he evoked hard for her to process. "Aurora needed to hear she isn't alone," she told him.

"I think you need to hear that, too. You aren't alone. I'm here." Reaching out, he tucked a strand of hair behind her ear.

Her body leaned into him and she caught herself. She'd always felt safe in his arms until he'd ripped the rug out from beneath her feet. Then again, she hadn't been much of an anchor for him, either.

"You're here for now. What happens when the next big adventure or opportunity comes calling?" She couldn't help but ask the question that lay on her mind.

He winced. "That's a fair question and one I deserve. Somehow I'm going to prove to you that I've changed and this is where I want to be. I learned a lot being away from the people I care about."

"It fits!"

Willow stepped away from Braden and turned to

Aurora. The too-large shirt had come from a mistaken purchase online at a no-return store, and she'd kept it. It hugged the girl's belly but didn't look too small.

"I'm using my own leggings because these didn't fit at all. But thank you." She held the black stretch pants out, and Willow folded them and put them back in her bag.

"You look great!" Willow noticed she'd brushed her hair and had color in her cheeks due to the excitement of going out.

Willow was grateful Braden had come up with this plan. She already liked Aurora and hated the idea of her living in a closet-sized room while mentally preparing to have a baby.

"Ready, ladies?" Braden asked, interrupting her thoughts.

"Are you sure your family won't mind the extra person?" Aurora twirled a strand of hair nervously around one finger.

"Positive. The more the merrier," he reassured her.

Willow wished someone would reassure *her* as she joined him and his huge family for dinner.

*   *   *

BRADEN THOUGHT HE'D have two women to worry about at his mom's house, but as it turned out, Aurora fit right in. Bri took an immediate liking to her, as if his twin sensed the young girl needed a friend. Given the wink Bri gave him, he figured she was also giving Braden time with Willow.

His mom always loaded them up on appetizers before a huge dinner, and Lord knew Aurora could use fattening up. Her and her baby, and after introductions, Bri hooked her arm in Aurora's and led her to the food table. It didn't escape his notice that Hudson joined them.

Willow was talking to Macy by the sliding glass doors leading to the patio, and it gave him time to study her. Listening to her tell Aurora about her past had been like a punch in the gut. Not only because he'd never been able to get her to confide in him that way but because of all she'd been through as a child.

Growing up, Braden had held a wealth of anger against his father for how he'd treated him, belittling his intelligence, mocking him for his inability to play sports as well as his siblings. But at the core of everything, Braden had a family who loved him. A mother who doted on each of her children and tried her best to cushion him from Jesse's emotional abuse, as did his uncle Paul. His biological dad, as he now knew.

Braden had had a roof over his head, people who loved him, and food to eat. He had a hunch there was much more to Willow's various foster homes than he knew. And he wanted to be the one she confided in, because he wanted to regain her trust. Since that wasn't going well, he needed to step up his pursuit in other ways and get her to remember what had been good between them.

He decided it was time to make his move and walked up to the two women who were deep in conversation. "Hi, ladies." He gave them his warmest smile.

"Hi there!" Macy said.

"Braden," Willow murmured, meeting his gaze.

"You two having a nice talk?" He knew Willow had been concerned about coming here today, but Braden's family would never leave her to fend for herself, and though he'd wanted to be with her, the women in his brothers' lives had stolen her away to get acquainted.

"We are," Willow said. "Macy was telling me about her sister and the custody fight she almost had with her half sister's mom."

"Who, by the way, has disappeared again," Macy muttered.

Braden placed a hand on her shoulder. "Jaxon told me how hard that was on you. I'm sorry Hannah won't know her mother well, but maybe it's for the best that you have nothing to do with a dysfunctional parent."

Willow shot him a surprised glance, her expression

quickly turning understanding. She'd known his issues with Jesse. They hadn't discussed his biological father reveal because he'd been away when that had occurred, and when he'd come home for Paul's kidney transplant, courtesy of Austin, Willow had no longer been part of his life.

Realizing he'd fallen into silence, he turned to Macy. "How's married life treating you?"

The pretty blonde his brother had fallen head over heels for while pretending to be in a real marriage smiled at him. "It's amazing. I honestly didn't think I could ever be this happy." She reached out and grasped his hand. "Marriage is the best thing that ever happened to me."

"I thought that was me." Jaxon appeared by her side, slipping an arm around his wife's waist and pressing a kiss to her cheek.

Braden wanted the right to kiss Willow any time or place, he thought, turning his stare her way. She was watching the happy couple, her face flushed at their open display of affection, naked need on her face.

He touched her hip, letting her know he was here. Aware of her feelings, that he was experiencing the same longing.

"I'm going to steal Willow," he said, grasping her elbow and pulling her away, heading to the side of the house with the guest bedrooms his mother had for her kids should they want or need to come home.

"Where are we going?" she asked, trying to slow him down.

"I want a few minutes alone with you." He slowed so she could more easily keep up.

He led her into his favorite guest room and shut the door behind them. Before she could argue or turn cold, he backed her against the nearest wall, braced his hands on her hips, and met her gaze. "How much longer are you going to keep me at a distance?"

Because he was finished giving her time when all it seemed to do was make her pull further away. That said, he'd take her on whatever terms she was willing to give, and he'd work his way back into her heart … because there was no place he'd rather be.

Chapter Six

WILLOW STARED INTO the gorgeous eyes of the most compelling man she'd ever met. For the last few hours, she'd been asking herself the same question he'd just posed, and the answer was obvious. She couldn't keep him at arm's length much longer. Not after seeing him at his kindest and warmest, caring for someone he'd met once. Looking out for a young pregnant girl and bringing her into his family. Pushing Willow past her own barriers and refusing to let her spend the holiday alone.

She couldn't resist him, but she couldn't trust him long term. Revealing her past to Aurora had reinforced Willow's fear of being left, and this man had done just that to her, the same way her mother, her father, and the homes she'd passed through had. But that didn't mean she was ready to turn her back on him right now. There was too much chemistry between them for her to ignore.

"I can't pretend I don't want you, Braden, but that doesn't mean I can have a relationship with you again."

Reaching up, he brushed her hair off her face, his calloused fingertips causing goose bumps to ripple along her skin. "Yet."

"I'm sorry ... what?"

"You can't have a relationship with me *yet*," he said, with all the self-assurance she expected of him. "I'll take whatever you can give me now, and we can build from there."

"I can give you friendship," she automatically said, her heart pounding inside her chest, knowing he wouldn't accept so little and aware deep down she couldn't, either.

A sexy smile lifted his lips. "We both want more." He slipped a hand behind her neck and paused, giving her a chance to pull away.

She didn't.

Couldn't.

And when his lips came down hard on hers, she was right there with him. His grip on her neck tightened, and she wound her arms around him, making certain they were as close as physically possible. His tongue swept over her lips, parted them, and plunged into her mouth. Ready and waiting, her tongue met his, and his unique flavor exploded inside her. Along with his seductive cologne, her body responded to everything about him.

His lips were soft, his kiss hard, as hard as the

body she shamelessly rubbed herself against. With a groan, he lowered his hands, slid them down her back until he cupped her ass and lifted her so she could wrap her legs around his waist. Once she secured her crossed ankles, he backed her against a wall to keep her upright, and she immediately felt the bulge of his erection pressing against her core.

She moaned, threading her fingers through his hair, their mouths never parting, making up for lost time. When she was in his arms, she was able to forget everything but him.

"God, I missed you," he said, his hips thrusting upward, causing sensation to burst forth inside her.

Not wanting to talk, she pulled on his hair, directing his mouth back to hers, and he was only too happy to comply. Kissing her again, he slid his hand up her shirt, his rough skin skimming over the bare skin of her belly and up toward her breast.

"Braden?" a male voice called out, and the sound of the door opening followed.

She jumped out of his arms and began adjusting her clothes at the same time Austin, Braden's oldest brother, walked into the room.

"What do you want, Austin?" Braden asked through clenched teeth. He reached for Willow, but she was too mortified to go to him.

"I need to… I mean excuse me," she said, rushing

past Austin and out of the room, heading to the bathroom, which she found next door.

Ducking inside, she shut the door and locked it behind her. She glanced in the mirror and discovered her cheeks were flushed, her eyes bright, and her hair messed from his fingers.

She blew out a deep breath and splashed cold water onto her face. "No regrets," she said to her reflection.

How else could she get Braden out of her system if she didn't let the passion play out? And oh my God, was there passion. Even more than she'd remembered. What was the expression? Absence makes the heart grow fonder?

She shook her head. No. Not the heart. Bracing her hands on the countertop, she ducked her head, came to a decision, and met her gaze once more. He could have her body but not her heart. She nodded her head at the thought. It worked for her. She'd spend nights with him when it worked for her and be a total professional during the day. And when she was finally over him, which she would be because he had left her, after all, she'd be the one to walk away.

Having made the decision, she felt a weight lift off her chest. Now she just prayed she was strong enough to carry out her plan and not fall for the man all over again.

She waited until her face coloring returned to normal and headed back to the party, finding Bri and Aurora and joining their conversation, pretending she hadn't just been making out with Braden in another room.

*   *   *

BRADEN WATCHED WILLOW bolt out of the room. Meanwhile his cock throbbed in his pants, and the evidence was obvious thanks to the bulge in his jeans. Not giving a shit that his brother was watching, he adjusted himself and glared at his sibling.

Austin pushed the door shut and shrugged. "Sorry, man."

Braden ground his teeth together. "Great timing, asshole." He finally had Willow where he wanted her, and Austin had to interrupt. "What do you want?"

Austin shoved his hands into his trouser pockets. "I didn't see you around and didn't realize Willow was missing, too. Figured I'd make sure you were all right. I know readjusting to being home can't be easy, and we haven't had much time to catch up."

"I was working on the hard parts when you interrupted," he muttered.

Austin, the older brother who'd always acted like a parent, braced his hand on Braden's neck. "How's it going?"

"Well, it was going great until you walked in."

Austin released him and rolled his eyes. "That's sex. How's it really going? You left her, right? And she wasn't exactly cozying up to you earlier in the main room. In fact, she was avoiding you entirely." He sounded serious, not like he was taking any pleasure in pointing out the fact.

With a groan, Braden flopped onto the bed. "She's still pissed. Doesn't trust me. I'm trying to take what I can get while showing her she can believe in me this time."

"And you think sex is the way to convince her?" Austin sounded surprised.

"Hey, it can't hurt to remind her of our chemistry while showing her all my stellar qualities at the same time." He would have laughed but it wasn't funny. "I'm working at proving myself, believe me."

Austin nodded. "That's all you can do. Meanwhile, it's almost dinnertime so let's go eat."

"Sounds like the best idea you've had all day." Because it certainly hadn't been walking in here, he thought, still frustrated because of the interruption.

They rejoined the family to find his mother had opened the chafing trays on the kitchen island for their buffet-style dinner. There were too many people for any kind of sit-down-and-be-served dinner. Damon had brought some teammates and there was a folding table set up in another room where the guys had congregated.

Braden looked around for Willow and found her across the room talking to Aurora, both women sitting, Aurora on a chair, Willow on an ottoman. He strode over to join them, catching Willow's gaze first and noting the flush that rose to her cheeks when she met his gaze, the kiss still alive between them.

"Am I interrupting?" he asked.

"Nope. We were just talking about … things," Aurora said, and he could sense her being deliberately vague.

He allowed her privacy. "Are you hungry? The food's out in the kitchen."

"We thought we would wait until everyone got theirs and then we'd go eat," Willow said.

He laughed. "Smart. I wouldn't want my hand to get between my brothers and food. Animals, the lot of them." He grinned, causing both women to chuckle.

"I'm going to the ladies' room before dinner," Aurora said, pushing herself to a standing position and centering herself before walking off.

"Everything okay?" he asked, taking the young woman's seat.

Willow nodded. "Can I ask you something?"

"Of course." He leaned in close, unsure what she wanted to say, but it sounded serious.

She glanced over her shoulder before turning back, seemingly satisfied. "About Aurora. I can't let her go back to a closet room in the back of a diner. I just can't." She looked at him with wide eyes as she said, "I want to let her move in with me."

He hadn't seen that coming but maybe he should have. Willow could obviously relate to her, and he'd known that when he'd made the decision to bring her with him to meet Aurora. But to have a stranger move in?

"Do you think I can trust her?" she asked on a whisper, as if reading his mind. "I realize that sounds awful, but I don't know her, and yet I can't let her live the way she has been."

He blew out a long breath. "Seems like you've already decided. And yes, my gut says you can trust her. But it's still a risk." One that worried him. Because really, what did they know about Aurora?

"Where will she sleep? You're in a one-bedroom." He'd move them both in with him, but he had no room, either, and there wasn't a chance Willow would agree.

She wrinkled her nose in thought. "My sofa is a pullout. I can sleep there. She can have my room. We travel quite a few more weekends, anyway."

He shook his head. "You can't—"

"I can. She's pregnant and looks exhausted, like

she hasn't slept. Did the bed in her room look solid?"

He ran his hand over his eyes. "It was a cot."

"Then that's that." Willow folded her arms across her chest, obviously determined. "Listen, I know what it's like to have no one. I can't imagine being her age and pregnant with no support system."

"And how will she get to work at the diner?"

"Oh my God, you're never going to believe this!" Aurora came rushing over, excitement in her voice. "Bri offered me a desk job at Dare Nation! She knows I only have a high school diploma, but she said I could answer phones and be trained. I don't have to stand on my feet all day taking orders anymore!" She covered her belly with her hand. "And I'll be making more money. There's a bus that goes from the diner to the area where Dare Nation is… Wait."

The bubble of excitement popped, and her shoulders drooped. "Merry may not let me stay in my room if I'm not working for her."

"I think it's amazing Bri offered you a job," he said. His sister had a big heart.

Braden met Willow's gaze. He really wanted her to take more time and think about the idea of Aurora moving in, but he saw exactly where this situation was leading. She hadn't gotten over her past, and that was pulling her to Aurora more deeply than he'd imagined.

"It's great," Willow agreed. "And I have a solution

to your living situation if you're interested."

Aurora's eyes opened wide as she listened to Willow's offer. The next thing he knew, the girl was crying in gratitude, Willow was hugging her tight, and Braden's throat grew full. This woman deserved the world, and he only knew that somehow he had to find a way to give it to her. To prove to her that he wouldn't fail her again.

After Aurora centered herself and was ready, they went to the buffet table and filled their plates. Aurora hesitated to load hers up, taking a tiny bit of turkey, sweet potato, and vegetable. Willow met his gaze, and he took over, grabbing the spoon and filling all three of their plates until the women were laughing and begging him to stop.

They wound up at the end of the dining room table his mother had added extensions to and settled in to eat. Aurora was across from them in deep conversation with Bri.

And Braden couldn't take his gaze off Willow, wondering how he'd ever get alone time now that she would have a roommate. He'd just have to cajole her over to his place. Or maybe he could finagle connecting rooms at their next away game, even though the last time was a fluke.

"How's dinner?" he asked, wanting to keep his mind off of how he could get Willow into bed.

"So good." She put a huge spoonful of sweet potato pie into her mouth and groaned, the sound going straight to his cock.

Thank God the tablecloth covered the front of his pants.

"So aren't you glad I showed up unannounced and saved your day?" he asked, eating but not paying attention to his own food.

"Okay, yes. I'm glad," she said, turning to the turkey and dipping it in extra gravy.

"And glad we came to an agreement?" he asked, speaking quietly, glad Quinn, who was on the other side of Willow, was busy feeding baby Jenny in the high chair. He didn't need an audience for this conversation.

She turned and met his gaze. "I'm not really sure what we agreed to."

He treated her to his best grin. "More of what happened between us earlier, that's what." And more emotional moments where he could cement their connection, but he wasn't about to tell her that and freak her out.

She swallowed hard. "I can handle that." She spoke softly.

His mother tapped a glass, calling for everyone's attention. "I'd like to say a few words."

Around the table, everyone grew silent.

His mom stood, tucking a strand of her dark hair with blonde highlights behind her ear. "It's a rare treat for me to have all my children home for a holiday, nobody off playing a game or rushing out on a work emergency, and today I'm grateful."

"We love you, Mom!" Damon called from beside his wife.

Everyone laughed and murmured agreements.

She glanced around the table, taking everyone in. "I want to welcome all our guests, as well. I'm so happy to have everyone."

Instinctively, Braden reached over, grasped Willow's hand, and squeezed tight, bringing it to his lap. This was what he wanted, her to be a part of his big, boisterous family.

His mom continued. "My family is expanding and I couldn't be more thrilled." Her gaze traveled to the new women in their world, Macy, Quinn, and Evie, ultimately landing on Willow and remaining for a few seconds.

A few too long. Because a glance at her profile told him his mom's words had been too much for her. She was suddenly stiff and looking around to escape.

Leaning over, he whispered to her. "Relax. Nobody's forcing you to marry me today," he said, giving her hand a reassuring squeeze.

And this time he didn't add the word *yet*. Although

he thought it.

His words did the job. She looked at him and rolled her eyes, grinning at his ridiculous comment.

"Of course, I wouldn't mind if all my children were settled." Thankfully, his mother then turned her gaze to Bri. She sat beside Hudson, who hadn't left her side for most of the afternoon.

Braden didn't have a problem with his best friend having a thing for his sister as long as Hudson had good intentions. The problem was, Bri didn't trust men outside her small circle of family.

"Do not go there, Mom. Marriage and babies don't have to be in everyone's future." She placed her napkin on the table and excused herself before walking out.

Hudson followed.

"Well, forget I said anything," his mom said and lowered her glass. "I meant well."

"She'll come back," Austin assured her as everyone else began quietly speaking again.

"What's going on?" Willow asked softly.

He groaned because Bri, like Willow, had her emotional walls high and for good reason. "Bri's been hurt before by men who have used her for her connections through Dare Nation or our brothers, who are in the sports world. It's going to take a man without an agenda to win her over."

"Makes sense," she murmured. "And Hudson? Do I sense an attraction there?"

"Looks like it to me. He has his work cut out for him if he's serious."

Willow met his gaze, her brown eyes full of understanding. "Then it looks like you have a lot in common."

Reaching out, he placed a hand on her leg beneath the table, squeezing her thigh. "Then it's a good thing I'm up to the challenge."

*   *   *

WILLOW HAD TO admit that the holiday at the Prescotts' had been fun. The women had all welcomed her and made her feel comfortable, as had Braden's brothers. Of course, she knew the teammates who'd come for dinner, and that had helped. And despite Braden's mother's push for the twins to settle down and her pointed look at Willow, the day had been a success. And the rest of the weekend was busy.

Willow insisted Aurora pack her things and move into her place immediately, and when she saw where the young girl had been living, she had no regrets or hesitation. The air conditioning barely worked in the back room, and Braden had been right. The room was the size of a closet, and ironically, it had none. Closet, that is. So Willow and Braden loaded up what little

Aurora owned and moved her into Willow's apartment.

Despite it being Thanksgiving weekend and the stores being extra crowded, she took Aurora shopping for clothes to wear to her new job, lending money, which the young woman promised to pay back as soon as possible. Willow didn't care as long as she knew she was helping someone in need. She loved watching Aurora blossom as she tried on new maternity clothes that fit and made her feel good about herself.

Because she and Braden weren't alone after Thanksgiving, they hadn't discussed that kiss or where they stood now. He gave her space, and when she saw him at the facility on Friday and Saturday, and at the home game on Sunday, he was professional as always in front of other people.

And through the week, though she expected him to corner her in her office or sneak time alone, he did neither. In fact, he seemed uptight, and when he didn't have patients, he left the facility altogether. Which led her to question if he'd changed his mind about pursuing her and wanting to prove he'd changed and would stay around. He wasn't the type to play games, so she assumed he really had been busy.

At home, despite Aurora's objection, Willow took the pullout sofa, and they settled into an easy routine. Willow left for work before Aurora woke, and the bathroom was in the hall, so Willow didn't have to worry about waking her up. She just picked her clothes out the night before. Meanwhile, Aurora took the bus to work, and Bri was getting her settled at the office.

This weekend was an away game, and Willow was packing a few extra things when a knock sounded on her door. She walked through her living area, which, considering it was now her bedroom, was well cleaned. Every morning she put the blankets and pillows she'd used away in the linen closet and made sure any of her clothes were in the hamper. Keeping her living area neat was a holdover from her days when she wanted the foster family she lived with to want to keep her with them. Even when she didn't like them all that much, the thought of starting over had always been daunting, and yet time after time, she'd had no choice.

Shaking her head, she checked the peephole and let Steffy inside. "Hi! How are you?" She shut the door behind her friend.

"Excited to be going to the game this weekend, roomie." Willow had put Steffy on the rotation. She was joining the team for the away game and they were sharing a room. When Willow was the only female trainer, she stayed by herself.

Willow smiled. "It'll be fun." She was looking forward to the short time away.

"You've been distracted all week. Care to tell me

what's going on?" Steffy asked, sitting down on the couch. "You've also been pretty quiet since Thanksgiving."

Joining her, Willow settled into a corner and pulled a throw pillow onto her lap. Since she'd spent the week letting her mind spin on what Braden wanted from her now that she'd decided it was time to give in, at least to their sexual desire, she turned to her friend.

Drawing a deep breath, she said, "I kissed Braden and I don't mean a quick peck on the cheek. I mean if we hadn't been interrupted, who knows where things would have gone between us."

Steffy's eyes opened wide. "Wow. Well, that's a big deal. So I get why you're distracted … but you don't seem happy."

Willow bit down on her lower lip. "I'm confused. I know I haven't told you much, but Braden and I dated for about a year, exclusively. Then one day out of the blue, he comes to me and tells me he's going to Doctors Without Borders for two years."

She remembered that day so vividly, sitting across from him in a café and him just blurting out the news as if it wouldn't have far-reaching repercussions for her. As if their connection to each other wasn't that important. "One day I'm thinking I have a guy in my life with the possibility of a future, and the next he says he's leaving. Just like that." She waved her hands through the air.

"Oh, wow. I had no idea. So what did you do?"

"I told him to have a good life and I walked out." Which, she admitted now, might not have been the most mature way to handle it. "Anyway, now he's back and he said he wanted us to try again."

Steffy leaned forward in her seat. "I need popcorn for this. It's like a good movie."

Willow could only laugh because her friend was right.

"And then what did you say?" Steffy asked.

Willow closed her eyes and sighed. "I told him I could only give him friendship. And then I contradicted myself by kissing him."

Letting out a whoop of glee, Steffy grinned.

"I'm glad you're enjoying this. I'm not, because he's been nothing but professional and friendly ever since his brother interrupted our kiss. I don't know what he wants from me and it's making me crazy." She rose to her feet and began pacing around the room.

"I wish we had time for wine, but we have to leave within the hour to catch the bus. So let's cut to the chase. What do _you_ want?"

Willow rubbed her hands together. "I can't bring myself to trust him not to leave me again, but I can't deny our attraction, either." The man was everything she wanted but couldn't let herself have, at least not long term.

"So indulge! I can't remember the last time I saw you do something for the fun of it. Or should I say do *someone*?" Steffy pushed herself up from her seat and walked over to Willow. "Nobody says you have to promise him anything. If he wants you and you want him, let it be that simple."

Nothing about Braden Prescott was simple. "He hasn't acted like he's still interested this past week."

"Probably because you've been at work, and he knows you'd never want your integrity compromised. But when we're at the hotel, who's to say you can't pay him a midnight visit?" She raised her eyebrows and wiggled them for effect. "Reach out for what you want, on your terms."

She let her friend's words sink in and decided Steffy was right. It was time to put her hurt behind her and indulge in the present. And since she'd put Braden through the paces since his return, it was up to her to make the next move.

*   *   *

TRAVEL DAYS SUCKED, Braden thought as he returned to his hotel room after dinner, washed up, undressed, and finally lay down on the king-size bed. He braced his hands behind his head, grateful for his own room on these trips. Up early, long flight to Dallas, and he'd had little sleep this week, his work and free time completely booked.

Every time he'd intended to find Willow, not wanting to let too much time pass and have her talk herself out of taking a step forward with him, something had interrupted. A player in need of a consult. Another doctor who wanted his opinion. A sibling who insisted on a quick lunch or dinner because it had been too long since he'd seriously caught up with anyone, keeping up with his own fitness routine, and then, of course, the health care center, where he'd worked long hours.

The best he could say about the clinic was that the place was in need of *more*. More supplies, more and better equipment, more nurses ... more of everything, and he was preoccupied with finding ways to fund the operation and get the people who frequented it better medical care. He had some ideas that needed fleshing out in his mind before he brought them to light with Hudson, but he was working on it. Just like he wanted to work on things with Willow.

He couldn't talk to her on the plane because she sat next to her friend and fellow therapist, and he wouldn't talk about their private affairs surrounded by the entire team, anyway. And when the keys had been handed out, he'd discovered she had a roommate this trip, which made paying her a late-night visit impossible.

Resigned to having to wait, he reached up to turn off the light and get some sleep when a knock sounded on his door. He rose from the bed and realized he'd left his clothes in a pile on the bathroom floor and had no pants to slip into.

He'd just check the peephole first, and if he had to let someone in, he'd get dressed.

A glance and his heart nearly stopped. In the hall, dressed in a pair of jeans and a tee shirt, hair pulled up with sexy strands falling around her face, and no makeup, just the way he liked her, stood Willow.

He glanced down at his boxer briefs and made a decision. If she was here now, she wasn't just here to talk, so he opened the door to let her in.

*   *   *

WILLOW DIDN'T GIVE herself a chance to change her mind about going to Braden's room. Right after dinner, she washed up and changed as if she were heading to a vending machine in the hotel in case she ran into someone on the way. Of course, that meant she couldn't dress up or put on a fresh face of makeup, she just had to go as is. It was the only way not to draw attention to herself and her destination. She'd lingered when they were passing out keys, making sure to get a look at the number written on the paper holding his key card. Nothing left to chance. She couldn't afford to show up at the wrong man's door.

Steffy didn't say a word, watching and nodding in approval as Willow prepared to go after what she wanted. More like what she needed. She and Braden had unfinished business, and she had every intention of putting a period on the end of their relationship. She wouldn't lie to him or lead him on. She had every intention of being up-front and honest with him. Since he was a guy, she couldn't see him turning her down.

Having made her decision, she refused to second-guess herself or allow for butterflies in her stomach as she grabbed her phone and made her way to the floor above her, stopping at his room.

She knocked and waited, catching herself in a lie. There were plenty of nerves and flutters in her belly.

The door opened and he stood in front of her, quickly pulling her in and closing them inside. One look at him and she knew why.

In his boxer briefs and nothing else, sweet Lord, the man was hot. He was even more muscular and ripped than he'd been before he left, and she couldn't tear her gaze from the six-pack that was his abdomen. His skin was tanned, and as her gaze fell to the happy trail leading straight into his waistband, the outline of his cock thick, hard, and evident, her mouth ran dry while her panties grew soaked.

"You can keep staring or we can talk about why you're here," he said in a gruff voice that sent tingles throughout her body.

"How can you answer the door practically naked?" She had a hard time lifting her stare and meeting his gaze. Not when the view was so damned good.

He treated her to a satisfied grin. "Because I saw it was you and I wanted to save us time. Unless you really did come to talk, in which case I'll get dressed. So which will it be?" He cocked an eyebrow and waited for an answer.

Chapter Seven

BRADEN KNEW FROM the flush in her cheeks he'd nailed her reason for being here, but she had to admit the truth. After chasing her for so long, a big part of him was relieved she'd come to him.

"No. Don't get dressed," she said, placing her phone on the nearest counter.

Her cheeks flushed in the way he liked to see when she was needy and aroused, and he withheld the urge to pump his fist. His cock was doing enough celebrating. He didn't need to piss her off, send her running, and lose this minor win. And he had no doubt she hadn't come to this decision lightly, nor did it mean all he'd want it to.

"But I do want some ground rules in place first."

He'd expected nothing less. "Name them."

She kept her gaze on his now and not on the bulge demanding attention. Hopefully he'd get some soon.

"For one thing, I don't want our relationship public at work. I have the guys' respect and I don't want to blow that."

He was tempted to remind her that Ian, her boss,

had met his wife at work and nobody had had an issue, but he kept his mouth shut.

He respected what she was saying and had no problem with the request. "Agreed. No PDA at work."

"Good. And it can't be like last time. It's not a relationship. We're … getting each other out of our systems."

On this he had a problem. A few, actually. "Permit me to modify your rule. First, we're exclusive or no deal," he said.

"Agreed," she answered immediately. "It's not like I want you bed-hopping while you're with me." She wrinkled her adorable nose in disgust.

"And you know better than to think I would." He was not, nor had he ever been, a cheater, and she knew it.

She blew out a breath. "Good. Now that that's settled–"

He shook his head. "I'm not finished." She wasn't going to like his next demand. And along with the no cheating rule, it was nonnegotiable.

Eyes narrowed, she folded her arms across her chest and waited.

"I want you to promise to keep an open mind about us. I want you back, and I'm going to do my damnedest to prove it to you."

She started to argue, and he placed a fingertip over

her soft lips before continuing. "I need to know you'll be open to my overtures. Let those walls down a little and see how good we can be together."

"That sounds like you're demolishing my second rule!" she said, ignoring his lingering finger, which he quickly removed.

He shrugged. "Because I am. Take it or leave it, sweetheart." Maybe it was arrogant, but he believed she'd accept his terms.

"You're turning down the offer of easy sex?" she asked in disbelief.

After she had her fit, he thought, suppressing a grin that would get him in trouble. "You bet I am, because I want more." He wanted it all, but that wasn't something she was ready to hear. "Well?" He reached a hand out toward her, wanting her to accept the gesture.

She bit down on her lip, and he could almost hear the debate in her mind before she placed her hand in his. "I'll try."

"That's all I can ask. Now come here and kiss me."

Next thing he knew, she was in his arms, her mouth on his. Bracing his hand on her face, he consumed her, finally tasting her and knowing it was just the beginning. He thrust his tongue into her eager and waiting mouth, the flavor of mint exploding inside.

She'd brushed her teeth in preparation. She'd come

here knowing she wanted to be with him. The thought did something for him in a deep and primal way.

He slid his hands to her ass and hauled her against him, and she moaned, the sound going right to his dick, but before he got her into his bed, he wanted to make this moment last. To remind her that there was so much more to them than just sex, and devouring her mouth in the hottest, wettest kiss showed her there was no rush to the end result. His cock disagreed, and the way she writhed against him, so did she.

She slipped her fingers into the waistband of his boxer briefs, cupped his ass in her palms, and held him tightly against her until she was rubbing her sex against his rock-hard erection.

He wasn't sure he could hold out, but he damned well intended to try. He lifted her shirt and broke the kiss to toss it over her head only to discover she was braless, and it was his turn to groan.

Cupping her breasts in his hands, he tweaked her nipples between his thumb and forefinger, remembering how sensitive they were and how she could get close to climaxing from that sensation alone.

She shuddered and leaned forward, pressing her face into the crook of his neck, kissing and licking his skin, all the while grinding her sweet pussy against the hard ridge of his cock, covered by too many clothes. Her soft hair tickled his cheek, the arousing scent of coconut invaded his nostrils, and his cock throbbed harder.

He needed them completely naked. Now.

"Strip," he said.

"You, too," she ordered as she kicked off her slip-on sneakers and unhooked the button on her jeans, then met his gaze and waited.

With a grin, he hooked his fingers into the waistband of his boxer briefs and pulled them over his straining erection before sliding them down and off.

She stared at his cock, desire filling her gaze. "I will admit I missed this." Reaching out, she wrapped her hand around his shaft and slid her palm up and down, swiping her thumb over the sensitive head.

"Jesus," he said on a hiss.

"Feel good?" she asked, not stopping her continual teasing with her hand.

Even better than his memories, that was for damned sure. He grasped her wrist, stopping her before he unloaded too soon. "Take off your jeans."

She wriggled out of the tight denim, leaving herself in the skimpiest pair of lace panties he'd ever seen.

"I suppose you want these off, too?" she asked, hooking her thumbs into the material on her hips and teasing him by not pulling them down, just wriggling her free fingers and all but daring him to come take them off himself.

"Unless you want me to rip them off."

Laughing, she began to slowly lower them.

This was what he'd wanted. A return to the light, teasing banter, the easy way they'd been with each other when things were good.

She let them drop to the floor and faced him, naked, so gorgeous she took his breath away. Her breasts round and full, her nipples tight and aroused, and there was a slight swell to her belly, which he'd always loved. Her legs were long and tanned, and then there was her neatly trimmed sex.

A low growl of desire escaped his throat. "Bed," he said, desire flooding his veins.

They didn't have far to go. Clasping her hand in his, he led her to the king-size bed in the center of his room, picked her up, and easily tossed her onto the middle of the mattress before climbing on.

He came over her and looked into her eyes. She immediately glanced away and grasped his cock, denying him the intimacy he sought, but he wasn't worried. He'd get his way soon.

As she slid her hand up and down his shaft, then moved to cup his balls in her hand, he groaned. He wanted to make this last, not come all over her like some teenager.

Time to tease her for a bit, he thought, easing himself down and spreading her thighs until he lay between her open legs. A glance at her glistening pussy and he was done for. Dipping his head, he slid his tongue through her sweet wetness and began to tease and torture her by licking around, near, and everywhere but her clit, where she needed him the most.

"Braden, please!" She gripped his hair in her hands and ground herself against his mouth.

Hearing his name on her lips was the best feeling, so he rewarded her by pulling the small bud into his mouth and working it with licks of his tongue and light grazing with his teeth. Her hips bucked and he placed a hand over her stomach, holding her down while he worked her over until she began to whimper, shake, and finally her climax hit. And though he wanted nothing more than to watch her come, he kept his focus on her pleasure and kept up the pressure until she was no longer writhing against him but overly sensitive. Only then did he lift himself up and glance at her face.

Satisfaction etched her features as her heavy-lidded gaze met his. "Gotta say that beat my vibrator."

He narrowed his gaze. "You no longer need to use that."

Although self-pleasure was better than another man providing her with relief. Hell, he didn't want to think about her with anyone else. Was he a hypocrite? Yes. And he didn't care to remember what he'd done in the last two years, because they'd meant nothing. He'd close his eyes and see Willow, and right after, he'd be filled with regret.

He rid his mind of those memories and focused on the woman before him. If he had his way, she would be the only woman in his future.

He grasped his hard cock and rubbed it over her clit. Her eyes dilated and she let out a moan. "I'll make you forget everything and everyone but me," he said, poised to enter her.

"Condom!" She lifted her head and met his gaze.

Shit. "Let me see if I have any in my bag." He'd known she was sharing a room and never thought she'd show up at his door.

She drew a deep breath. "I'm still on birth control."

Without getting into his recent past, he said, "I was tested for everything when I got back."

Sudden uncertainty filled her gaze, and he waited for her to come to a decision.

* * *

WILLOW'S BODY STILL quivered with a combination of satisfaction and need as she and Braden discussed protection. And though she was the first to offer up the fact that she was on the pill, she quickly came to the realization of just what she was getting herself into.

Being with Braden bare skin to skin was a step toward intimacy she wasn't sure she was ready to take. On the other hand, she didn't want to get into the discussion that would be even more serious if she admitted to her reservations. Reservations that were only about her heart. She trusted him to keep her safe this way.

Making her choice, she asked, "Then what are you waiting for?"

He studied her for a moment, and she knew he was wondering what she'd been thinking.

She didn't want to talk. "I want you, Braden."

"You have no idea how much I need you." He came over her and covered her mouth with his, kissing her like he needed her to breathe.

Sex between them had always been amazing, but his current intensity took things to another level. She kissed him back, shoving all negative and worrisome thoughts out of her mind. Instead she concentrated on Braden, her hands rubbing over his back, savoring the feel of his warm skin against her palms.

With his hands on either side of her head, he rose up, and though his mouth never left hers, his cock slid back and forth along her clit. She trembled, the feel of his velvety-soft erection sending sparks of fire throughout her body. She craved him inside her, hard, thick, and filling her completely.

It was her turn to confess her need. "Fuck me,

Braden," she said, arching her hips and begging him to take her.

He lifted himself up and met her gaze. "It's been too long, so this time I'll give you what you want, but make no mistake. I am going to make love to you, too."

Her mouth dropped open and he grinned, a sexy, heart-stopping smile. And then he was at her entrance, working his way inside. Although wet and aroused, she gasped at his thickness and groaned.

He paused and she had no choice but to meet his gaze. "It's been awhile, okay?"

He held himself steady, the veins in his biceps straining with his weight. "How long?"

"Unimportant. Move," she said, diverting her gaze. She bent her legs, pulling him deeper, her insides pulsing with desire.

"Babe, look at me."

She had no choice. "What?" she asked, staring into his gorgeous eyes. Eyes that devoured her.

"I need to know."

"There's been no one since you," she admitted, hating how that sounded. Like she'd been pining for him.

"There's not going to be anyone else," he said on a growl, thrusting inside her and pausing.

She lowered her hands, grasped his ass, and pulled

him against her. "Do not stop."

Once freed from the leash he held himself on, he began to thrust hard and fast inside her. He filled her, pulling back and plunging back in. Over and over he took her, the sensations building every time. Unfortunately so did the emotions and feelings she'd been holding back. He didn't need to make love to her in order for her to remember them. When they were good. Happy. A couple.

And as her inner walls clasped him tight, he moved faster, thrust deeper, taking her higher. It didn't take long for her to feel the beginning of her orgasm, and she let out a low moan.

"That's it, come for me. Come hard," he said, slamming back into her.

"Braden, oh! God," she cried out. His cock hit exactly the right spot inside her, and she came apart, white spots behind her eyes, a roaring in her ears as pleasure consumed her.

She rode out her orgasm, and only when he'd wrung everything out of her did he pick up his pace with short, fast strokes, and soon he was coming, too. His body shook and her name was on his lips.

She wasn't sure how long they lay with him on top of her, breathing heavily, perspiration coating their bodies, before she came back to herself. She opened her eyes just as he pulled out of her and rolled to his back.

"Jesus." He rested his arm over his head and groaned. "Best ever," he muttered.

She didn't respond despite the fact that she agreed. "C'mere," he said, reaching for her.

"I should get back to my room. We have an early morning." Leaving before they curled up together was the only way to keep some semblance of emotional protection, her promise to keep an open mind be damned.

He tipped his head toward her. "Don't run."

She drew a deep breath and swallowed hard. "I'm not. I just feel like it's smarter on the road not to call attention to us."

He frowned like he was going to argue but finally pushed himself to a sitting position. "Does that mean you'll stay over once we're back home?"

She shook her head and couldn't control the laugh that escaped. He was like a little kid who would try every which way to get what he wanted.

"How about we'll see?" She hadn't said no, so she could at least claim to be keeping an open mind, she thought wryly.

Taking her off guard, he pulled her into him and wrapped his big, warm body around hers. "I'll take it," he said, pressing open-mouthed kisses against her neck.

She had no doubt he'd hold her to her promise, and though she said she'd consider it, she had no doubt he'd convince her to stay over one day soon.

She finally dressed and walked out of Braden's room. Leaving him in bed, she shut the door behind her.

"Willow!" The sound of Cole's voice startled her, and she glanced up to see him stepping into the hall from a few doors down, ice bucket in hand.

"Hi." The need to run her hand through her definitely messed hair was strong, but she refrained.

"I didn't know you were on this floor."

She bit down on the inside of her cheek. "I'm—"

Before she could come up with a reply, the door behind her opened, and Braden joined her in the hall ... in his boxers. "You forgot your phone," he said gruffly, his gaze coming to rest on Cole. "Everything okay?"

Cole narrowed his gaze. "I see you didn't take my advice not to get involved with him."

She stiffened. "I don't see how that's any of your business."

Braden's hand came to rest on her shoulder. "I agree."

Willow didn't know what Braden's expression was behind her, but Cole shook his head, turned, and went back into his room, slamming the door behind him.

She flinched at the sound, and Braden turned her to face him.

"You do realize you're still nearly naked?" And she couldn't tear her gaze away from his gorgeous body.

He pulled her back inside and shut the door. "I know that's the last thing you wanted. Someone from work knowing you were with me tonight."

She sighed. "He already knew we had history. I just don't get what his problem is or why he's so angry. He and I weren't serious."

Braden raised an eyebrow. "He lost, sweetheart. No man with a healthy ounce of ego likes to know he came in second to another guy. Especially regarding a woman as sexy and special as you." He ran his knuckles down her cheek, and she shivered at the sensual touch.

"Thank you," she said, a rush of heat rising to her face. "Still, he's acting like an ass." And if he continued to give her a hard time, she'd be having words with him.

A troubled look crossed Braden's features. "I don't like him trying to get between us by planting ideas in your head that don't need to be there."

Ideas about him leaving again, she thought. She didn't need Cole reminding her of what Braden was capable of, having already lived through his unexpected departure once before. A subject she didn't want in the forefront of her mind. It was always there, lingering.

"Don't worry about Cole. I can think for myself," she assured him, her tone a little cooler than she'd intended.

Besides, the last thing she wanted was for Braden to get into a male pissing contest with Cole since they worked together. Or rather, Cole answered ultimately to him.

"Good." His lips lifted in a satisfied smile, which made her relax a bit. "Now kiss me good-night."

"I already did." But she wouldn't mind another long, wet, drugging kiss to keep her warm for the rest of the night.

Reaching up onto her tiptoes, she met his lips with hers, and he gave her exactly that.

*   *   *

BRADEN STOOD ON the sidelines watching the game. He still hadn't gotten used to the sound of clashing helmets and the roar of the crowd from this close to the action, but the play was fascinating from his vantage point. As the hours passed, he became more aware that Willow made a concerted effort to remain far away from him, on opposite sides of the bench, unless an injury on the field brought them together. He understood and had no problem with respecting her boundaries. Not as long as he knew he had a shot.

He glanced over to see her retaping a player's ankle while Cole smartly kept his distance from them both, his focus on his job as it should be. The Thunder won thirty to twenty-eight, Damon having his best passing yardage total of the season so far. Braden considered the weekend a success.

They flew home that night, and next Sunday was a home game, which meant more rest and less stress. Willow sat beside Steffy on the plane.

Braden joined his brother in the seat next to him and buckled his seat belt. "Good game."

Damon leaned back against the headrest, turning to meet Braden's gaze. "I have to say it feels great to be back and playing in top form with that damned scandal behind me."

"Can't say I blame you." He checked his phone, grinned, and typed something in.

"Evie?" Braden guessed.

Still smiling, Damon nodded.

"Why the fuck are you grinning like the Cheshire cat? You're creeping me out."

Damon leaned closer. "Evie's pregnant. We're keeping it quiet for now because it's still early, but I need to tell someone or I'm going to explode."

Now Braden understood his brother's great mood and shit-eating grin. "Congratulations, man. I am so happy for you. Give Evie my best. If you tell her I know she's pregnant, that is."

Damon's expression turned to one of horror. "Are you kidding? She'll kill me. She wants to wait until after the first trimester."

Braden chuckled. "Something tells me you won't make it till then. And you know Mom's going to lose her mind."

"Which is why we have to wait." Damon was adamant.

"She won't hear it from me," he promised.

"So what's the deal with you and Willow? Austin said he walked in on you two at Mom's over Thanksgiving." Damon changed the subject on him.

Braden rolled his eyes at his gossiping brothers.

Unable to help himself, he turned and caught a glimpse of her in an aisle seat, laughing at something her friend had said. As if sensing his stare, she looked his way, their eyes meeting. He winked at her, she blushed, and after he grinned, he turned back to Damon.

"Okay, talk," Damon said.

"I'm working on her, okay? It's going to take time for her to trust me again." Braden had no intention of revealing last night to anyone, not even his brother. Not against Willow's wishes. This wasn't anything like Damon being unable to contain his excitement about becoming a dad and spilling those beans.

Damon stretched his legs in front of him, as far as they would go given the boundaries of the seat in front of him. "And Aurora? The pregnant girl you two brought to Mom's? Bri seems to have taken her under her wing by giving her a job."

"So has Willow. She insisted Aurora move in with her, and given where the girl was living before, I couldn't exactly argue. Although that wasn't in my plans when I introduced them." He rolled his shoulders, feeling cramped in the small area. "I admit I brought them together because I thought it would help Willow and Aurora both. They have trust issues in common."

"And Dr. Do-Good couldn't help trying to fix them?" Damon cocked an eyebrow, annoying Braden.

"No. I needed Willow to see me in a new light and help Aurora at the same time." He let out a groan. "I just want her back without the distrust lingering in the back of her mind. She thinks I'm going to up and leave again."

"Are you?"

He shook his head. "When I left, I was looking for something, though I didn't realize it at the time." He cleared his throat. "I needed to carve out a niche that was mine. Not in the shadows of the successful Prescott athletes."

Damon turned to him. "I had no idea you felt … what? Less than us? God damn Jesse," he muttered.

Stiffening at the mention of the man who'd raised him, belittled him, and yes, had put those inadequate feelings in his head, he clenched his teeth hard. But Damon had a point. It always came back to Jesse Prescott.

"It's fine. I'm over it. Doctors Without Borders helped me with finding myself. Goal accomplished." He knew who he was, his place in the world, and in the family now.

Damon studied him as he spoke. "And have you explained this to Willow?"

"No." Braden groaned, rubbing his hands over his eyes. "If I bring up the time that I left, she pulls away. I'm lucky she's giving me the little that she is." He paused, needing to explain more but constrained by Willow's desire to keep their relationship a secret.

Fuck it, he decided, he needed his brother's advice, and Damon would be discreet with anything Braden told him. And he was certain Steffy knew where Willow had disappeared to last night.

"Okay, here's the truth but keep it to yourself. Willow doesn't want the team to know. She came to my room last night. She's willing to sleep with me, but she intended it to be a friends-with-benefits type of thing. Not a relationship."

Damon let out a low chuckle. "Been there, done that," he muttered. "What'd you say?"

"Hell no. If she wanted me, she needed to agree to keep an open mind and give us a chance." Damon opened his mouth to speak and Braden held up a hand. "Don't worry. I know she's full of it. She's going to keep her walls high." He blew out a huff of frustration.

"Take it from someone who's been in your position. It just takes time. The longer she's with you, the more she gets to know you again, the harder she's going to fall." He slapped Braden on the shoulder. "Hang in there."

"I intend to."

Chapter Eight

WILLOW ARRIVED HOME and found Aurora watching television on the couch that substituted for Willow's bed. After dragging her carry-on into the apartment, she shut the door and locked it behind her.

"Welcome home!" Aurora rose from the couch and immediately began folding up the blanket she'd been lying under.

Willow smiled. "Relax. I need to unpack and wash up before I can even think about using the sofa bed." She wanted the young woman to feel comfortable here, not as if she was in the way. "How was your weekend?"

Sitting back down and leaning against the sofa, Aurora smiled, and for the first time since Willow had met her, it reached her eyes. "Amazing. I relaxed in a comfortable home and bed." Gratitude filled her gaze. "I don't know how to thank you."

Willow joined her on the sofa. "Just seeing you looking rested is enough. And work?"

"Work was amazing. Sitting at a desk is a blessing

compared to waiting tables, and I'm really learning things. One of the secretaries is teaching me Excel, and it hasn't been too hard answering phones and transferring calls." She sighed and her happiness was real.

"Have you thought about what you're going to do after the baby is born?" Willow asked gently. She didn't want to bring up uncomfortable subjects, but they were important.

Placing her hand on her stomach, Aurora shook her head. "I mean, yes, I've thought about it. No, I haven't come up with any solutions." She rubbed her belly, tears in her eyes. "I want to keep her. I just don't know how I can."

Willow placed a hand over hers. "I didn't mean to upset you. We'll talk about it when we have more time. But I have to ask. What about the baby's father? Does he know you're pregnant?"

Aurora shook her head hard. "It was a one-night thing. I don't even know how to find him. And I never knew his last name." She blushed at the admission.

"You are not the only woman to get pregnant from one night. And don't beat yourself up over it, honey. Let's get some sleep and we'll talk more another time." Meanwhile she'd look into federal subsidy programs and other options for single moms. Although, one way or another, Aurora would need child care while she worked.

"Thank you, Willow." Reaching over, Aurora wrapped her arms around Willow and hugged her tight. "I'll give you your bed," she said, pushing herself back and standing up. "Oh! How was your weekend?" she asked.

Which part? Willow wanted to ask. Her time with Braden? Hot, incredible, and better than she could have dreamed. Keeping her expectations in check was going to be even more difficult than she'd hoped. "The game was great. If you didn't watch, the Thunder won."

"I saw! It was a fun game." She was standing now, folding the blanket. "It's amazing having a television to watch, too."

Willow smiled. "Let me do a quick unpacking in the bedroom, and then I'll be out of there."

After tossing her dirty clothes into the laundry basket and grabbing pajamas to sleep in, she washed up in the bathroom. To her surprise, Aurora had pulled out the sofa bed and set up her extra pillows and comforter she kept in the closet.

By the time she lay down, she was already exhausted from a long weekend of travel and game day. Not to mention she'd tossed and turned after leaving Braden's room the night before, pleasurable memories consuming her.

Before she could relive the time in her mind yet again, her phone buzzed, and she reached over, picked up the phone, and checked the screen.

Braden had texted her. *Did you and Steffy get home safely?*

She wrote back, *We did, thanks.* She wasn't used to someone looking out for her.

The other night meant something to me.

She sighed. It had meant something to her, too, but she hesitated on how to answer, and he replied again before she had. *Sleep tight. See you tomorrow.*

She typed back, *Night, Braden.* She sighed and put her phone on the end table beside her make-shift bed, knowing her alarm was set for the next morning. Though she expected to toss and turn and worry about what was going on between herself and Braden, to her surprise, she fell right to sleep, and when she woke up, she felt rested.

She performed her morning routine and rushed out to the team facility in order to work on everyone's pulled and stiff muscles and injuries from the game. As per usual on a Monday, her day was jam-packed, as were all the trainers on staff.

She didn't see Braden, which meant he was tied up with more serious injuries and filling the coaches in on each situation. By the time she had a few minutes for lunch, it was two o'clock.

She gestured with a tip of her head for Steffy to join her, and they locked themselves in Willow's office for a few blessed minutes of peace and quiet. Unfortunately it didn't last long, and soon they were back working with the team.

By the time she grabbed her bag to head home, she was exhausted. The parking lot was devoid of people but filled with cars of those still working. She approached her vehicle, about to hit the open button on the key fob in her hand.

"Working late?" Cole popped out of seemingly nowhere, from between two cars, one next to hers.

"You scared me." Her pulse sped up and she placed a hand over her chest. "Where did you come from?"

He'd walked around her and stood beside her car as he tipped his head toward where he'd come from. But neither was his vehicle and she narrowed her gaze. "I need to get going."

"You shouldn't walk to your car alone. It's not safe." He leaned against her Ford Focus, blocking her way.

Cole, who'd always been an easygoing guy, was starting to frighten her. "It's perfectly safe. There's a security guard at the entrance to the lot," she said, as much to remind him as to reassure herself.

"I used to walk you out," he said, his gaze never

leaving hers. "Is your new boyfriend too busy to be bothered?"

"Braden isn't my boyfriend. And nothing about me is your business anymore. Now if you'll excuse me, I want to get to my car."

Taking his time, he stood straighter and walked toward her. She held her ground, and he stepped aside only when he would have knocked into her.

She didn't know what kind of game he was playing but she didn't like it. And though she didn't want to, she glanced over her shoulder to make sure he was walking away, only to find him watching her.

A shiver raced through her, and she unlocked her vehicle, climbed in, and locked the doors behind her, letting out a relieved breath. Maybe it was a coincidence he'd been standing by the cars ... even if it seemed like he'd been waiting for her, but he'd shaken her up anyway. She had a hard time believing Cole was dangerous, but his behavior was odd at best, stalkerish at the worst.

Once she calmed down, she pulled her car out of the spot, avoided driving by the facility's side entrance, not wanting to see if Cole still stood watching her. Instead she took the long way to reach the guard station.

She relaxed on the highway home, and by the time she parked her car and entered her apartment, she'd decided Cole was just put out about Braden and had acted out of character. It was best for her to put the incident behind her.

The apartment was empty, and she caught sight of a note on the small kitchen table. Aurora had gone to visit Merry, her old boss, and her husband. She wouldn't be home for dinner, something Willow hadn't given a thought. She'd been away over the weekend, and the food in the fridge wasn't fresh since she usually grocery shopped on Saturday morning.

A glance in the fridge told her she was wrong. Aurora must have gone shopping, because the inside was filled with healthy food. Looking in the freezer, she saw premade store-bought meals she could heat in the microwave. From the amount of food, Aurora had obviously bought for two, probably wanting to do something to pay Willow back. And though she hadn't had to, Willow appreciated her efforts especially since she was so hungry.

She took a quick shower and grabbed her clothing for tomorrow from her bedroom. Wearing a pair of matching pajama shorts and a tank top, she opened the freezer to take out an easy meal when the doorbell rang.

She padded over in her bare feet and suddenly remembered her run-in with Cole. Worried he might have decided to pay her a visit, she glanced in the peephole, relieved and surprised to see Braden's face.

Opening the door, she realized he had a pizza box in his hand. "Braden! I'm so glad it's you," she said, expelling a sigh of relief.

Curiosity and concern etched his features.

"Were you expecting someone else?" he asked, brows furrowed.

"I– No." She didn't think he needed to hear about her run-in with her ex. "What is this?" She gestured to the delicious-smelling food in his hand and asked, despite it being obvious.

"I thought I'd surprise you and Aurora with dinner. I called but no one answered your cell. Hopefully I'm not too late?"

He looked like a hopeful boy with his sheepish grin, but in truth he was all man in his gray sweats, which, it went without saying, showed off his attributes. His Thunder tee shirt hugged his muscles. And the day's growth of beard gave him a scruffy, sexy appearance. His hair was messed as if he'd been running his hands through the strands, and if he'd had a day like she had, she understood the desire. She had the impulse to touch the soft strands, too.

She cleared her throat. "Actually you're just in time. Come on in." She waved him inside and locked the door behind her, unsure if she was happier to see him or the food. "But Aurora is out. She left a note she went to visit Merry, the woman who owns the diner where she used to stay."

"I remember." He headed directly for the kitchen and placed the box on the counter. "So this means I get you all to myself." He sounded pleased by the prospect, and she couldn't deny she wasn't too upset herself.

"You do." She opened a cabinet and reached for plates, setting them down on the table while he picked up the box and set it down in front of them. "Let me see what we have to drink. Aurora went shopping while I was away."

She returned with two cans of ginger ale. "Obviously she's caffeine free," Willow said with a grin. "Or would you prefer water?"

"This is good." He grabbed napkins, and they settled in beside each other at the round table. "Just like old times," he said, treating her to a sincere smile.

He was too sweet, and she didn't want to come back with a snarky answer about their past. "It is," she said instead.

He put a slice of plain pizza on her plate before taking one for himself. Obviously he remembered she was fussy and didn't like any toppings.

"I barely had time to grab a protein bar for lunch today," she said, picking up the slice and taking a huge bite. She didn't care how it looked, her empty stomach needed food.

"Same here." He took a bite, too, chewed, and swallowed.

"So excuse me if I devour this," she said, taking more.

He chuckled and ate in silence. Finally, three slices later and she wasn't even embarrassed, she felt full. He'd finished as well, and she quickly cleaned up, with him helping her, and they moved to the couch in the den.

She sat down and he settled in, turning to face her. Sensing he wanted to talk, she did the same.

"So, I know the season is crazy, and there'll never be real downtime," he began.

Wondering where he was going with his train of thought, she remained silent and waited for him to continue.

"I was hoping that we could still find time to catch up." He shook his head. "No, that's not right. Actually I hoped we could talk about ourselves and things we didn't get into last time we were together. I want you to know me this time. And I want to know you." He reached out and grasped her hand, running a thumb over her skin.

She swallowed hard. "You already know a lot," she murmured, nerves bouncing around in her stomach because this kind of emotional intimacy was hard for her. Harder still because both things he wanted to discuss brought up painful memories for her.

A wry smile lifted his lips. "Not really. I didn't know the details you told Aurora about how you grew up. And you don't know why I left, something I didn't realize until I was gone."

"Braden–"

"We don't have a real second chance without truth and honesty between us," he said in a roughened voice.

Was that what she wanted? she asked herself. A real chance at a future? Even if it meant being willing to open herself up and be vulnerable? Or did she want to do as she'd promised herself, have sex and keep her heart to herself?

*　*　*

BRADEN WAITED FOR her to reply, knowing the fate of their relationship and any kind of future depended on her answer. He'd given them a lot of thought since their night together. Considering the football season commitments and work, wining and dining her would be difficult but he had every intention of trying. And sex was amazing, and of course he wanted her in his bed, but unless she opened up, their chances of succeeding as a couple was slim. He needed her on board.

He looked into her big blue eyes as she nodded. "Okay, but I can only handle one of those big subjects at a time."

He reached a hand out, brushed her hair off her shoulder, and cupped her cheek. "That works for me, beautiful. What do you want to talk about first?" He dropped his hand onto his lap and waited for her to choose.

He hoped she'd pick their relationship so he could explain what he'd learned by going, taking time away from his family, the career he'd been building, even and most importantly, leaving *her*.

"So about my childhood. Obviously, it's not something I like to discuss because it means I have to remember a really painful period in my life, and it wasn't just a short period of time."

He slipped his hands into hers and waited for her to talk.

"You heard what I told Aurora, that my mom didn't pick me up from school one day. But I didn't tell her about the time before then. Or each place I lived before the Jonases'." She began to pull her hand back and he held on tight. "Why does this matter?"

He raised an eyebrow. "Because it goes to the core of why you don't trust, that's why. And because I want to know all of you." It was the only way they'd truly connect the way they needed to, he thought.

"Okay." She exhaled a deep breath and kept her gaze on their intertwined hands. "My mother wasn't interested in being a parent, so I guess you could say she emotionally abandoned me long before she actually left."

"How so?"

She lifted her legs and wrapped her arms around them, not meeting his gaze. "She brought men home. Different men."

His gut churned as she began to speak, anger filling him on behalf of the little girl she'd been.

She released his hands. "And she'd lock me in my room while they were over. Sometimes she'd forget to give me dinner because she was busy putting her face on, as she called it, so I went to bed hungry. But I usually couldn't sleep, and I could hear them through the paper-thin walls of the apartment. I guess you could say I learned early on my feelings and what I needed didn't count for much."

His hands curled into tight fists. Maybe it wasn't fair to make her relive these moments. "Willow, on second thought–"

She shook her head. "No. You wanted to know? I'm going to tell you." Drawing a deep breath, she went on. "One day, Mom didn't pick me up from school, and after I spent the afternoon at the police station, a woman from social services showed up to take me to my temporary home. Until they found my mom."

"Except they didn't," he said, stomach twisting with pain for her.

"Nope. And that began my rotation of foster families." Her legs slid back down to the floor with a thud, and she faced him again. "Some were decent, some were in it for the money, some had too many kids, most weren't all that interested in our lives. If social services needed to add a younger child to a home, I'd get bumped to someone who'd take older kids, sometimes with no notice. Just pack your bag and let's go. And by bag I mean trash bag."

He winced and, for the first time, looked around her small apartment, really taking in his surroundings. The couch was generic, one you could find in any retail store, the pillows matching, but there were no personal mementos. No photographs of family or friends, nothing he sensed had sentimental value.

The desire to fill her place with warmth and family gripped him and wouldn't let go. She deserved so much more than she had in life, and knowing she was sleeping on the sofa so Aurora would have a comfortable bed showed him she gave more than she took. Or expected.

"Enough," he said in a gruff voice. "It hurts to hear how you grew up."

"But isn't that what you wanted? To know everything?"

He nodded. "I just didn't know how much it would break my heart." Grasping her wrist, he pulled her toward him, and she came willingly, her body falling on top of his.

"I need to hold you." He needed to make her forget. Hell, *he* needed to put her story somewhere where it wouldn't hurt.

He shifted positions until they were comfortable and he was stretched out on the couch, Willow's sweet body cushioned on top of him. And then they were making out, his tongue sweeping through her mouth, desire pulsing through him. His cock throbbed against her core, and when she shifted her hips, she moaned.

Never breaking the kiss, he worked his hand between them and slid his fingers into her flimsy shorts and panties, finding her soaking wet. She rolled to the side closest to the cushions, giving him room to play. He dipped his fingers lower and spread her arousal around her sex, teasing her with long caresses and not so innocent pinches that had her squirming and arching into his hand.

"I wish we could go into the bedroom," he said, his throbbing cock knowing it wasn't going to get any relief tonight. But more because he wanted to make love to her and soothe her after he'd forced her to relive the memories.

She shook her head. "It's Aurora's bed for now, and no way do we have time to change sheets after. It's making out like teenagers or nothing."

He nipped at her bottom lip. "I'll take the making out, but next time you're coming to my place."

"No arguing there," she murmured, surprising him with how pliant and willing she was in his arms. "Now hurry up and make me come, because I don't know when Aurora will be back, and I want to have time for you." Her eyes gleamed with naughtiness.

Obviously she'd put the heaviness of their conversation behind her, something he assumed she'd learned how to do. Compartmentalize the pain so she could survive.

He refocused on Willow, gliding his fingers over her pussy back and forth, until he inched his way to her clit. A full-body shudder told him she was close, and he began to rub her in easy circles until she grabbed his wrist and positioned his palm exactly where she needed pressure.

She arched her hips and rolled her sex against his hand. A glance at her face showed him flushed cheeks and lightly parted lips. So beautiful, he thought, and refusing to disappoint her, he rocked his hand back and forth, taking her higher. His own erection strained against his sweats, but he ignored his need in favor of hers.

Suddenly she cried out, stiffening as she came. He pressed and circled his hand harder as she rode out her orgasm, the satisfaction he gained from watching her come and giving her pleasure beyond anything he could have imagined.

She grew lax against him and sighed, obviously sated as he ran his hand back and forth over her hair. "Your turn," she said, her fingers walking their way over his shirt, pulling the hem out of the way.

He groaned, and just as her fingers were about to inch beneath his sweats, the sound of keys in the lock jolted them to action. Willow rolled off him and maneuvered into a sitting position while he did the same, pulling a throw pillow from the chair beside them over his lap. No way did he want Aurora getting a view of his dick.

They glanced at each other and grinned. Knowing there was no way to hide what they'd been up to, he braced himself.

"Hi," Aurora called out as she let herself in. The door slammed and locked behind her, and in a few steps, she caught sight of them on the sofa. "Oh! I didn't realize you had company. And I'm interrupting. I'm so sorry."

"It's fine. You're fine." Willow rose to her feet, something much easier for her to do than him. "How was your dinner?"

"Nice. It was good to see Merry." She glanced at Braden and blushed.

"I'm glad you're keeping in touch with her," he said, not wanting Aurora to be uncomfortable.

The young woman smiled. "Umm, I'm going to wash up and get ready for bed," she said, quickly excusing herself and rushing into the bedroom.

Braden cleared his throat. "I think I should go," he said, finally rising and getting rid of the pillow.

"Sorry about that." Willow looked at the bulge in his pants.

He grinned. "I'm not. I got to make you come," he said in a low voice. "Well worth the discomfort."

Willow shook her head and walked him to the door. "Thanks again for dinner."

"Thank you for opening up to me." It was an amazing start. He stepped closer and kissed her lips. "Come home with me after work tomorrow? You can follow me home, stay over, and leave before me," he said, before she could come up with a work excuse. Like not wanting to show up at the same time and get people talking.

She hesitated and he wondered if he'd pushed too fast.

"Okay," she murmured. "I'll put an overnight bag in my car."

He felt as if they'd taken a huge step tonight, and he was beyond hopeful for the future.

*   *   *

After Braden left, Willow convinced Aurora to come out of the bedroom and hang out with her for a little while. Willow hadn't opened her bed yet, so they could sit on the sofa and relax. They'd done this a couple of times this week, and Willow had begun to enjoy the company. Of course, she had Steffy and their wine nights, though they hadn't had one of those in a while, but she liked her talks with Aurora, too.

"Before I sit down, I'm going to grab some ice cream. Want some?" Willow asked.

Aurora's eyes opened wide and she smiled. "Oh my God, yes. I had a big dinner but I'm craving sweets." She sat down on the couch and placed her hands over her growing belly.

After raiding the freezer, Willow returned with two pints of ice cream and two spoons. "I say we just call dibs and enjoy. Cookie dough or cookies and cream?"

"Cookies and cream."

She handed over the pint and a spoon, then settled in cross-legged on the cushioned couch. She took off the top, took a huge spoonful, and moaned. "I am so glad you left me the cookie dough."

Aurora laughed. "You should have just said which

one you wanted."

Willow shrugged. "I like both but I do love cookie dough. So how's it going at Dare Nation? I know it hasn't been long, but you're enjoying it?"

"So much. I finally feel like I might have a normal life. Well, there's the baby issue but I'll figure something out."

In her last trimester without a plan, a permanent place to live, or a daycare lined up, time was running out, Willow thought. She'd done some looking into subsidy programs, and with the money Aurora was making by working at Dare Nation, she probably wouldn't qualify. But that didn't mean she could afford everything she needed on her own, either.

"I know that look. Can we not talk about me tonight? How's Braden?" Aurora asked, changing the subject.

Fine. She'd give in for now. "Braden is good. We're getting to know each other again." She'd told Aurora about their history and how she was hesitant about the future.

Although she could talk to Steffy, only someone who'd shared similar pasts to Willow could relate to her feelings. But there were age and life experience differences between her and Aurora, which made it hard for the younger woman to understand completely. Regardless, Willow felt a sisterly connection with her.

"I like him," Aurora said. "He's a good man. His whole family. They're decent people."

"They are," Willow murmured. She dug into her ice cream and took a cold spoonful.

Memories of Braden bringing her a brownie sundae surfaced, and she squirmed in her seat, her sex still tingling from her earlier orgasm. Not the time, she reminded herself, focusing on Aurora.

"But they don't understand me the way you do."

Willow glanced over, surprised. She'd just been thinking the same thing. But she wanted Aurora open to new and caring people. "They want to help and I'm glad you let them."

"I don't know how I got so lucky, but when I met Braden, my life changed."

"Mine, too."

They sat in silence, eating their ice cream until they'd both had enough. Aurora rose and took both of their containers and spoons into the kitchen to clean up, and Willow stood, ready to get some sleep.

Aurora walked over and paused. "Willow, I'm really glad I have you in my life," she said and went in for a hug, her belly stopping her and they both laughed.

"I'm glad I have you, too." A warm feeling stole over her, knowing she had someone in her life who truly felt like family.

Chapter Nine

LATER IN THE week, Willow massaged the ankle Damon had twisted at Sunday's game, impressed that his conversation centered on football and not Willow's relationship with his brother. She appreciated his discretion at work and focused on easing his pain and making sure he could play this week.

"Come back tomorrow for more stim and therapy," she told him. It was Thursday and they had time. "We'll wrap it Sunday and you should be good to go."

"Love your magic hands," Damon said, winking at her.

"Leave my girl alone and go home to your own," Braden said, joining them and smacking his brother on the head.

At least one brother was discreet, she thought, shooting him an annoyed look.

"You're so easy to get going." Damon eased himself off the table, chuckling the entire time.

Even Willow grinned.

"Austin!" Damon waved at their brother, and Willow turned to see the man dressed in a suit and tie, ever the professional agent, joining them. "Here to talk to your star player?" Damon asked.

Braden rolled his eyes. "He doesn't just represent you, remember? Arrogant son of a bitch," he said with no bite, just a grin.

"As much as I'd like to stay and joke like we did when we were kids, I need to have a serious talk with Braden and Willow."

She blinked, surprised. "About what?" What would Austin want with her?

"Is everything okay?" Damon, the one left out, asked.

Austin nodded. "It's nothing about our family."

Damon's stiff shoulders visibly relaxed. "I'll leave you all to it then." He walked off, favoring his ankle.

"Ask Steffy to wrap that ankle before you go home," Willow called out to him, and he answered with a thumbs-up over his shoulder.

Austin glanced from Willow to Braden. "Do you have someplace private we can talk?"

"My office." Braden lifted a hand, clearly intending to put it on her back before realizing where he was, and gestured toward the exit instead.

Once they were in Braden's office, which, unlike Willow's, had personal touches – photos of his family and matching desk accessories—Austin closed the door.

Worried, she couldn't wait a moment more. "What's wrong?"

"I wouldn't say anything's wrong," Austin said. "It's just that I had a visitor at the office this morning. A man named Lincoln Kingston. He's based in New York." Austin braced a hand on the desk as he spoke. "He claims to be Aurora's brother."

"What?" She shook her head in denial. "No. Aurora's mother left her with her grandmother, and she died when Aurora was five. She spent her childhood in foster care." Willow narrowed her gaze, not understanding. "And why would this man come to you?"

The brothers exchanged glances that Willow took to mean they were worried about her reaction, but she didn't care.

"I know you're protective of her but let Austin tell us everything." Braden wrapped an arm around her waist, pulling her close.

His body heat calmed her somewhat. She just didn't want the young woman scammed or hurt more than she already had been. "Sorry. Go on."

Austin nodded. "It's a long story, but apparently there are four Kingston siblings, and believe it or not, you've probably heard of them. Dash Kingston–"

"The rock star?" Shock ripped through her.

Austin nodded. "It gets better. Xander Kingston, the actor, and there's a sister, Chloe."

"I don't believe this. Where the hell have they been all her life?" Braden's voice rose in anger, and Willow's heart squeezed tight at his protective reaction that mirrored her own.

"I'll tell you if you'll chill out," Austin said.

It was Willow's turn to hug Braden back and calm him down.

"We're listening."

Austin settled on the corner of the desk, his expression thoughtful as he spoke. "Their father died recently, and as the son in charge of the family business, it was left to Lincoln to go through his paperwork. He found monthly checks to a woman they didn't know dating back over eighteen years. All had been cashed."

Braden let out a whistle. "That's a red flag," he muttered.

Nodding, Austin went on. "Exactly. He had a private investigator do some digging. They found the woman, and she admitted to having an affair with Charles Kingston and getting pregnant. Charles wanted her to end the pregnancy, but she insisted on keeping the baby, so he paid her to keep it quiet. He didn't want his wife and family to find out."

"Wait." Willow stiffened, feeling herself getting worked up all over again as she thought about the implications of the story so far. "Are you telling me she gave the baby to her mother, Aurora's grandmother"—because that's what the young woman had told Willow had happened—"and then she took off but continued cashing the checks? Not giving anything to her kid?" she asked loudly and in utter disbelief.

"Yes." Austin eyed her warily, obviously waiting for another tirade to kick in, but she wanted to hear the rest, so she drew a deep breath and let it out before speaking. "Did she know her mother had died?"

Austin nodded.

"And she never went back for her daughter?"

She already knew the answer since Aurora said she never saw her mother again, but there was a slight chance there was something she didn't know about.

"Unfortunately, no," Austin said.

She felt the weight of Braden's stare, knowing he watched her carefully, but she couldn't focus on him right now. Anger rushed through her, but she held on to her temper, knowing getting visibly upset would get her nowhere.

"So this woman just let her daughter end up in foster care." Willow spun out of Braden's grasp and stalked to the window overlooking the parking lot.

The cars blurred as her eyes filled with tears, just thinking about what Aurora had lived through while her mother did God knows what with money that could have changed the young woman's life. Of course, having her mother would have been better, but like Willow's mom, Aurora's hadn't cared.

Willow wrapped her arms around herself and turned toward the men.

Braden took a step toward her, but she shook her head. She wanted the facts, not comforting. "What else did her mother say? And how did they track Aurora to you?" she asked Austin.

"At first they hit a dead end, what with the grandmother passing away and Aurora aging out of foster care and disappearing. She didn't come up on any of the obvious checks. Driver's license, social media, credit cards, et cetera, until she took a job with us."

"Aah. That makes sense," Braden said.

"Since Bri insisted we pay Aurora a week up-front so she had something to live on, as soon as she opened a bank account and cashed the check, the private investigator had something to go on. And they traced her to Dare Nation."

If this story was true, then the Kingstons were looking for Aurora, and they wanted her to be part of their family. But they didn't know anything about these people, and Willow wanted to protect the girl who'd come to mean something to her.

"And you're sure it's legitimate?" Braden asked, echoing her thoughts.

"Evie is looking into everything," Austin said of his and Braden's sister-in-law and Damon's wife, who was a private investigator. "But I have faith it's all true. They went searching for the sister they didn't know they had. It's not something a family with money would do lightly unless they cared."

Willow nodded, her shoulders slumping in relief. "Do they know Aurora is pregnant?" Would that change how they felt about her?

"No. I didn't think it was my place to tell them."

Braden inclined his head. "Good call. Until Evie knows for certain their story checks out, we don't tell Aurora anything about this. Agreed?"

"Agreed," Willow said. This would be a huge shock, and she wanted to make sure everything was true first. Then they'd sit her down and give her the shock of her life.

"Does Bri know?" Braden looked to his brother.

"Yes, but she won't say anything," Austin assured them. "Meanwhile, he's staying at the W Hotel and is waiting to hear from us on when he can see her. I have to tell you, he didn't take it well that we didn't just give him easy access, and I was lucky Aurora was out to lunch with Bri when he showed up. He has every intention of convincing his sister to come back home with him and be part of the family."

Willow's mouth opened, then shut again.

"Thanks, Austin. We appreciate you coming over," Braden said, obviously speaking for her because she was too shocked to reply herself.

Austin started for the door and grasped the handle before turning back and glancing at Willow. "Are you okay?" He glanced at her, concern in eyes that were so similar to Braden's.

Startled by his thoughtfulness, she forced a smile. "I am. I just want what's best for her." Which was true. She'd just grown to care about Aurora, and the thought of her leaving was sudden and shocking. "Thanks for asking," she murmured.

Austin winked. "We take care of our own," he said, opening the door, walking out, and shutting it again behind him.

"That's my brother, stealing all the good lines." Braden's voice caught her attention, and she turned toward him.

He held out his arms, and she walked into them, drawing on his strength and body heat. She buried her face against him and inhaled his masculine scent.

"You're upset because he wants to take her back with them, aren't you?" he asked.

She nodded and took a step back. "I know she hasn't been with me long, but I care about her and I like having her around." She bit down on the inside of her cheek. "But if these people really are her family, it would be selfish of me to want her to stay."

"Hey. The last thing you are is selfish." Braden brushed his knuckles over her cheek, and she trembled, her nipples tightening at his light touch.

She appreciated his kind words, but there was a hint of honesty in what she'd said. Still, it didn't matter what Willow wanted. "The truth is Aurora needs this to be real. Once she has the baby, she won't be able to afford an apartment, daycare, and everything else it takes to live. She keeps avoiding the conversation and I don't blame her. But if these people are her family? If she comes from money and they want to bring her home?" Willow shrugged. "That's a win for her."

He nodded. "Evie will have answers soon and we'll go from there. Besides, even if she decides to go to New York with them, and we don't know that's the case, it's not like you can't FaceTime or visit."

She managed a smile. "I know. It just feels like a loss is coming."

He grasped her hands just as a knock sounded at the door. Looking annoyed at the interruption, he released her. "Come in!"

The door opened and Cole stepped into the room, his gaze encompassing them both.

"If you two don't mind, there are patients out there who are more important than your personal lives."

Braden stiffened and narrowed his gaze. Willow wanted nothing more than to touch him and calm him before things escalated, but anything she did would only make things worse, at least from Cole's perspective.

When neither of them moved, he eyed them with disdain and annoyance.

"Who needs me?" Braden asked in a tight voice.

"Devon White. And James Slater is waiting on you," he said to Willow, his gaze lingering on her in an unnerving way.

"Tell Devon I'll be out in a few minutes."

Cole's fingers gripped the door tighter. "And what about Willow?"

From beside him, Willow could feel every muscle in Braden's body tightening. "She'll be right there. Now please leave and close the door behind you."

When Cole didn't move fast enough, Braden strode over and did it for him, pushing the door back and forcing him out.

She winced, knowing Cole would not take being dismissed well. "I'm not sure that was a good idea. And he's right. I should get out to my patient."

Braden turned the lock on the door and walked back to her. "One, I can't stand that bastard. Two, you don't answer to him, and three, I sure as shit do not take orders from someone who works for me." A muscle ticked in his jaw from the tension Cole had created.

She blew out a long breath. "I know. But–" She hesitated, wondering if she should mention his stalker-ish behavior or if that would work Braden up even more.

"But what?" He braced his hands on her shoulders and forced her to meet his gaze. "Talk to me."

She sighed. "It's probably nothing, but the other night, I walked out to the parking lot by myself, and Cole was there ... lurking near my car."

Braden let out a low growl, his body vibrating. "I'm going to kill him."

"And that's why I didn't tell you when you came over that night. I knew you'd overreact and–"

"You saw what he just did." He gestured between them and the door. "The way he behaved? I'm not overreacting. And I'll be walking you to your car," he said under his breath.

Now wasn't the time to argue, so she held her objection back. The fact that he cared enough to make sure she was safe carved out another space in her heart. She couldn't remember the last person who protected her in any meaningful way.

"Thank you." She rose onto her tiptoes and brushed a kiss over his lips, but before he could grab her hips, she danced back out of the way. "We really need to work."

"But you're coming home with me tonight," he said, a hint of vulnerability in his voice. As if he were worried she'd changed her mind.

How could she? He was becoming more and more important to her as the days went on.

*   *   *

As BRADEN WENT through the rest of his day, he couldn't take his eyes off Cole, and his blood boiled inside him. He treated his patients, though it was no surprise to him there'd been no one looking for him despite Walsh's claim to the contrary.

He'd had a brutal day, seeing players and meeting with coaches all afternoon. Today was his day off at the clinic, and he couldn't help but worry if they were short-staffed there. And after the emotionally draining meeting in his office with Austin and Willow, he wanted nothing more than to head home and climb into bed with his woman. But first he had something to take care of.

Braden deliberately stayed later than the rest of the doctors, trainers, and therapists, making sure to schedule Cole's appointments late, as well. He sent Willow a text saying he'd be there in ten minutes to walk her out so she could follow him home. Then he made his way to the training room, where Cole was getting his things together to leave for the day.

Making sure no one was still around or liable to intrude, Braden walked up behind the man. "Walsh!"

Cole jerked in surprise and spun around, eyeing Braden warily and for good reason. He'd been waiting for this moment all day.

"You and I need to come to an understanding." Anger vibrated inside him, and as Braden stepped closer, he realized not only was he broader but taller than Willow's ex.

And from the look on Cole's face, he realized it as well and backed himself against the wall, away from Braden.

"I don't have anything to say to you."

"Yeah, well, I have something to tell you. I hold your job in my hands. One word to Ian and you're out." He started out with the threat he hoped would mean the most to the man.

"Not unless he has cause." He puffed up his chest like he'd made a valid and irrefutable point.

"Yeah? How's stalking a female employee? Is that cause?" Braden asked, taking a step closer.

Cole's face flushed red. "That's bullshit."

"And yet somehow I think Ian will believe Willow over you." Annoyed with the asshole who couldn't take a hint, Braden tried yet another tactic that kept his hands clean. "Listen, man. I don't have a problem with you as long as you leave Willow alone." He deliberately caged Cole against the wall. "Do you understand?"

"She was mine until you came along." His whiny voice didn't make his point. He trembled but didn't back down.

Braden shook his head in disgust. "You ought to learn how to read a woman better. Consider that man-to-man advice. Now, are you going to back off?" He really hoped the prick said yes.

"Fuck you. I'm not doing anything wrong."

Braden snapped. He grabbed Cole around the neck, not hard enough to hurt him or leave bruises, but the action made his point, and Cole's eyes grew wide in his pale face.

"I may be a doctor like you, but I grew up with big-ass athletic brothers who knew how to fight. You don't want to get into it with me." He paused to let his words sink in. "If I hear or see you bothering her again, you'll answer to me. And you won't just lose your job." He released him and followed up with a shove against the wall. "I mean it, Walsh. She doesn't exist for you."

He walked away without looking back and headed for Willow's office so they could go home.

*   *   *

WILLOW MADE HERSELF comfortable at Braden's

apartment while he showered. He'd said they would order in dinner, but while he was busy, she explored the kitchen, hoping she could find ingredients to cook for him. Unfortunately his refrigerator and cabinets contained typical bachelor fare. Some canned soup and boxes of macaroni and cheese, cereal, milk, and beer.

"Oh well." She laughed at her findings and walked through the living room, exploring the items on the wooden shelves on either side of the large television.

Just like in his office, there were photos of his family, including a picture of his mother, a man she assumed was the father who'd raised him, and all the kids when they were young. She wasn't surprised to see a more serious-looking Braden wearing glasses, standing beside his twin, while the other boys acted out. One had his tongue out; another put his fingers up in rabbit ears over Bri's head. They were adorable, and she ran her finger over the glass, glad he'd had his siblings growing up.

"We were all a bunch of goofballs," he said, coming up behind her, his body warm from his shower.

He smelled like the masculine soap he used, and she turned around and practically face-planted into his bare chest, he was so close. Taking advantage, she breathed in deep, inhaling the scent that aroused her so deeply before stepping back.

She met his gaze and devoured him with her eyes.

Between his damp, finger-combed hair, the gray sweats that were made to show off his attributes, and his muscled chest and arms, she couldn't stop staring.

His lips lifted in a knowing grin.

"Have a good shower?" she asked, ignoring the fact that he'd caught her ogling him.

He nodded. "I needed one. The day just felt too damned long."

She narrowed her gaze. "You've been off since you came to my office. Want to talk about it?"

He hesitated and then said, "I gave Cole a piece of my mind along with a warning." He eyed her warily, as if he knew she wasn't going to like what he'd just said.

And she didn't. "I don't think it's a good idea for you two to get into it at work."

"I was careful but he needed to be put in his place."

She nodded, unable to deny that Cole had been acting irrationally and unprofessionally. "What did you say to him?"

"Basically I let him know he's been out of line, and if he doesn't cool it, he'll be out of a job." He shrugged. "I also might have told him to stay the hell away from you. Or else."

She groaned, imagining how Cole would react to threats. "Aren't you concerned you might push him over the edge? He's definitely not the rational man I thought he was."

He braced his hands on her forearms. "He needed a warning and I'm pretty sure he got the message."

Deciding she didn't want details, she accepted Braden's explanation. "Okay. But you don't need to fight battles over me. I can handle him."

"But you shouldn't have to. Now what do you want to do for dinner?"

"It's not like you have anything for me to cook for us, so how about … Mexican? Sushi? What do you prefer?"

He tucked a strand of hair behind her ear. "You choose. I didn't invite you here to cook."

"But I would have. Do you ever go shopping? You can't live on takeout," she said, taking his hand and leading him to the sofa.

"Between the clinic and work for the team, I have no time. Let me grab my phone and we can order. You pick." He kissed the tip of her nose and walked away, leaving her to stare at his ass, hugged by his sweats.

In the end, they ordered sushi – a variety of rolls, mostly chef's specials that sounded delicious and edamame as an appetizer. Now they sat on the sofa waiting for dinner to be delivered, with her in her favorite cross-legged position, facing Braden. They talked easily about a variety of things, from work and player injuries to how little free time the season provided them. The one thing they didn't discuss was the situation with Aurora, because until Evie verified the Kingstons' relationship with her, there wasn't anything they could do.

"Tell me about the clinic," Willow said. "I know you met Aurora there and you're busy with patients but I'm curious."

His gaze warmed at the question, but his brows furrowed, and she could see things weren't great there.

"Unfortunately it's a shit show. Hudson and I are frustrated. We don't have all the equipment we need to treat people. We run short on PPE, the sonogram machine is ancient, and half the time we don't have an X-ray technician because they can't afford to pay one." Obviously discouraged, he uttered a low groan.

She moved closer and settled in his lap. "You care so much. I wish I could help."

He ran his hand through her hair, the feel of his fingers tugging the long strands delicious.

"I just appreciate your interest. Would you like to come see the place?" he asked.

She nodded, excited. "I'd love to. When?"

"I say we escape during lunch tomorrow. We'll head over and I'll give you a quick tour, introduce you to Thomas Anderson, the doctor who runs the clinic."

"Actually, I'm off tomorrow. I haven't had a day to myself in forever. I figured I'd do things around the apartment."

A playful grin teased his lips. "I think I'll let Hudson know he can handle things, then. I'm playing hooky with you. We can go for breakfast, I'll take you to the health care center, and maybe we can even end up on the beach. What do you say?"

She sighed, done fighting herself. She was going to enjoy this time with him … really enjoy. Not keep reminding herself of the past. She'd deal with his leaving if and when the time came. There wasn't much more he could do to prove he cared, and she desperately wanted to be with him while she could.

"I say let's do it."

"Yes." He grinned and captured her lips with his.

At the first slide of his tongue into her mouth, she moaned and kissed him back. Eager to taste him. Eager to grab on to him while she could. His hand came up and cupped the back of her neck and held her in place while he plundered her mouth, leaving no doubt how much he wanted her.

She pulled at the hem of his shirt, lifting it up and rubbing her palms against his muscular abdomen, soaking up his warmth, sliding her hands upward.

The sound of the phone dinging jarred her out of the sensual haze she'd been lost in while he leaned his head back and groaned. "Dinner," he muttered. "They'll be ringing the bell any minute."

She pushed herself off him and stood, waiting while he did the same. A look at his erection straining against his sweats and she grinned. "I think I'll get the door."

He adjusted his cock and she knew he had to be uncomfortable. "Yeah. Good idea," he muttered, clearly annoyed by the interruption.

But her stomach grumbled, and she rushed for the door just as the bell rang.

*   *   *

BRADEN WOKE UP cuddling a soft, warm body in his arms, and he took a minute to savor the feeling. Last night was the first time he and Willow had spent the entire night together since reuniting, and he could now see why his brothers had fallen hard and fast when they realized they had found the one woman meant for them.

Something had changed with Willow, and he didn't think it was his imagination. She'd lowered her guard, let him in, and he was so fucking grateful. He saw it in her easygoing manner, her faster smiles, and her curiosity about his life. And he'd felt it the minute he'd slid into her body, her wet heat clamping down on his cock and emotions rushing through him. But he'd really known everything had changed when he'd looked into her eyes without encouraging her to meet his gaze. She hadn't held back.

Since he knew he'd scare her with the words, he kept them to himself. It was enough that he knew. Telling her would come when she really believed he was here to stay. They were at the fragile beginning, but he'd made progress.

She stirred in his arms and rolled to her back, her sleepy eyes fluttering open and meeting his gaze. "Morning."

He leaned over and pressed a kiss to her lips.

"Nooo. I haven't brushed my teeth." She laughed and slid out of bed.

"I don't care," he called after her, his gaze on her naked back and ass as she walked into the bathroom.

Rolling over, he groaned. His dick was already hard, and it wasn't just morning wood. He waited for her to finish and slipped out of bed next, taking care of business and laughing as he brushed his teeth before rejoining her in bed.

He rose on top of her and kissed her in earnest. Last night he'd tasted every inch of her body. He'd sucked on her tight nipples, licked and nipped at her breasts, and spent plenty of time teasing her pussy before thrusting his tongue inside, pinching her clit, and making her come.

Now though? He wanted to go slow and make sure she felt everything he did. As he pushed into her, his gaze locked with hers, and he slowly eased himself so deep she gasped as he bottomed out inside.

"You feel that? That's me, right where I belong. So deep you don't know where you end and I begin."

He thrust upward once more before gliding out, taking his time with each and every slide. She moaned, arching her hips, and he made sure to grind himself against her clit before pulling out again. Slow and steady, wanting her pleasure to wash over her while he watched.

She'd wrapped her arms around him, and suddenly she blinked, a tear leaking from one eye.

"Am I hurting you? Should I stop?" He began to pull out, and she lowered her hands and gripped his ass.

"Don't you dare. It's just … so intense, so good," she said, urging him back into her.

"That's because it's us," he said as her palms pushed him deeper and she squeezed her inner muscles around him.

The combination triggered him, and he began to thrust, pounding into her faster, harder, and deeper than before.

"Yes, Braden. Harder," she said on a frustrated sob.

She clamped around him, causing sensation to shoot through him. His balls drew up tight, but he was alert enough to know she had to come first and he had to watch her while she came apart beneath him. He lifted himself up and changed his angle, searching for just the right spot inside her that would send her soaring.

"Oh God, yes!" She arched her hips and suddenly stilled, then her entire body began to shake as she came … and came, the orgasm ripping through her and seemingly going on forever.

He gritted his teeth and continued to hit that spot, as her fingers found his shoulders and her nails dug deep. He forced his eyes open, watching her flushed cheeks and startled expression. Just as she loosened her hold, her climax obviously easing, he picked up his pace and chased his own orgasm that didn't take long to hit.

He came, losing whatever had been left of him to the woman in his arms.

Chapter Ten

WILLOW BOUNCED IN the passenger seat of Braden's car, vibrating with excitement at the prospect of seeing the health care clinic that meant so much to him. Their night and morning had been more perfect than she could have imagined, and she was so glad she'd let herself go and just enjoy. She'd forgotten how good they were together and had been doing her best not to let herself remember.

The truth was, they were even better now. Each of them was at a good point in their own career, they had so much in common, and he obviously cared for her. There had been no doubt in her mind he wasn't just having sex, he was making love. She'd felt his feelings with every fiber of her being.

Now she just had to hope he meant what he said. That he was staying and couldn't be lured away again. That he wouldn't leave her behind for something bigger and better, making her feel like she still wasn't enough.

She shook her head, clearing her thoughts, reminding herself of her promise to live in the here and now.

She was giving him a real chance.

Relaxed, sunglasses on, he drove her through an obviously depressed part of town, taking her deeper into an area where people struggled, and it made her sad. She knew what it was like to be hungry, and though she'd helped Aurora, she couldn't take in everyone who came into the clinic or who had problems.

"We're here." He'd pulled onto a non-paved parking lot and parked the car.

Subdued, she followed him inside.

The center was quiet, which he assured her was not usually the case. The beige walls were dingy and added to the depressing look of the place overall.

But Braden's excitement as he showed her around and introduced her to the man who ran the center was contagious. The receptionist called in sick and their nurse had quit. Still, it was obvious there was so much good that could happen here if only they could get more funding. They spent an hour at the center, giving Braden a chance to fill out some paperwork and look up information on a few of his patients.

While they were there, a mother came in with her two children and a crying infant, and since Dr. Thompson was busy with one of his regulars, a diabetic older man, Braden stepped in.

Though Willow waited, sitting in a chair in a nearby office, the walls were thin, and she heard Braden's deep voice talking to one of the little girls. The baby had stopped crying, and she thought she heard the mother say she'd nurse her so Braden could focus on her other child.

"Can I look at your throat?" he asked in a gentle voice she'd never heard from him before. Maybe the girl nodded because Braden's next words were, "Open your mouth wide and say aaah."

"Aaah."

"Looks red with some white postules. Probably strep. I'm going to run a test, okay?"

A little while later, Braden had correctly diagnosed her, prescribed an antibiotic and Children's Tylenol, did his best to assure the mom that the medicine was generic and wouldn't be too expensive. She already had Tylenol at home. He gave the little girls lollipops and sent them on their way but not before telling them to come back if the infection didn't clear up.

His kind demeanor brought a lump to her throat. This was the man she hadn't wanted to dig deep enough to know because now she was falling hard despite her attempts to keep him at a distance. God, she hoped he didn't disappoint her or it would destroy her.

Finally, he stepped into the room where she waited. "I'm so sorry. I didn't expect to take care of anyone today."

"It's fine," she said, rising from her seat. "I totally understand." She smiled and he grinned back. "Ready to go?"

She nodded. They said goodbye to Dr. Thompson and headed back to the car. Once inside, she buckled up, and he turned on the engine, hooking up his cell.

She was about to ask him how she could help with the clinic when his phone rang.

He glanced down, his eyebrows raising at the number, and he accepted the call. "Adam Niles, I'll be damned. It's been awhile."

Braden shot her an apologetic look but she waved off his worry. She didn't mind if he took a call from someone he obviously was surprised to hear from.

"Hey, Braden. How are the States treating you? Enjoying all the comforts of home or do you miss us down here in Brazil?"

Willow stiffened then forced herself to breathe. Braden was entitled to talk to friends from his time with the relief organization. It didn't mean he was leaving. Only her mind immediately went there, she tried to reassure herself.

Braden glanced her way before answering. "I'm happy to be home," he told the other man. "How's it going?"

"We're good." He went on to tell Braden a story

about one of their colleagues marrying a nurse he'd been dating and talked about the vaccinations they were focusing on giving to the villagers nearby.

It was obviously a long-distance call and one he couldn't easily return if his friend was in the field, so Willow stretched her legs out and waited while he talked. It was clear Braden felt a connection to the man on the phone and the people Adam updated him on.

On the surface, everything was normal, a typical call, two friends catching up, but Willow couldn't stop her stomach from churning with nerves. The call reminded her of the times the phone would ring in her foster homes, and from the way her foster mom or dad had looked at Willow, she knew bad news was coming.

Telling herself it was all in her head, she took deep breaths and waited patiently.

Finally the other man wrapped up his end of the call. "Well, it was great talking to you."

"Same here. Say hi to the team," Braden said.

"We all miss you, buddy," Adam said before clicking off.

Braden disconnected the call and immediately turned to her. "Sorry about that. I haven't spoken to him since I left."

"It's fine." She wrapped her arms around herself,

trying to find her center. "So what's next on our agenda for the day?" she asked with a forced smile. She was determined to enjoy their time together.

No matter what her unwarranted panic attack told her.

* * *

AFTER THEIR TRIP to the health care center, Braden drove them back to her place so she could put on her bathing suit, and since he'd had his trunks in the car, he'd changed at her place, too.

She walked out of her bedroom in time to see Braden in his swim trunks, pulling a tee shirt over his head. His tanned, lean stomach and the six-pack that showed he worked out had her drooling.

Meeting her gaze, he grinned. "See something you like?"

"Put your ego away," she said, laughing.

He stepped closer, grabbed her around the waist, and pulled her against him. His rock-hard erection told her that if she wanted to skip the beach, he'd probably be all too willing. But he'd promised her a special day, and she intended to see what he had planned.

"I'd like to see what's beneath that cover-up. The lace is just a tease," he said in a gruff voice.

"And that's all you're going to get until we're at the beach." She spun out of his arms and picked up the tote bag she'd packed, giving him a wink over her shoulder.

She liked this side of her, the light, easy side he brought out. It had been too long since she'd let go, if ever.

As they drove downtown to South Beach, he slid his fingers into hers and rested their coupled hands on his muscular thigh, and she relished the small intimacy. She glanced out the window and saw the sun shone brilliantly overhead. Palm trees and expensive cars lined the street, and people walked on the sidewalks, browsing in store windows. She closed her eyes, enjoying the ride and the way they could be together in peaceful silence without it feeling awkward in any way.

He signaled to pull the car into a garage, and she opened her eyes at the sound. "Where are we?"

"It's a garage to the apartment building Ian lived in before he and Riley had kids and moved. He kept the place and it's on the beach. He lets family use it when they want a day to themselves." Braden parked the car and met her on her side, helping her out.

As they made their way to the pool area and the beach beyond, she took in the private cabanas and the people sunbathing on beach chairs, some under umbrellas, others soaking in the rays. Something she wanted to do herself.

"Are we sitting on the beach or out here by the

pool?" she asked.

"Lady's choice."

She lifted her sunglasses and looked around. "Would we have one of those cabanas?" she asked.

He nodded. "We would."

"Hmm. I love the sand but this pool looks like heaven," she said of the infinity-edge pool.

"But the cabanas have curtains that can give us complete privacy inside." He met her gaze and, like her, raised his sunglasses, giving her a view of his seductive indigo eyes. "I mean, think of the things we could do in there," he said in a husky voice.

"Decision made. Poolside it is."

He strode over to the hut that supplied towels and where guests checked in, returning along with a young man who set them up at two poolside chairs far away from other people, clearly at Braden's request. Behind them was their private cabana.

She kicked off her sandals and pulled off her cover-up, revealing the suit she'd chosen to put on while Braden changed in her bathroom. She'd wanted to surprise him, and from the expression on his face now, she had. The strappy red bathing suit with discreet cutouts both covered her appropriately and revealed hints of bare skin. A glance down showed her that his cock was thickening behind his bathing suit trunks, and an answering rush of desire filled her in return, making the prospect of them using that cabana highly likely.

After towels were placed on the chairs and tucked in, and the attendant tipped and gone, they settled on their chaise lounges, the plush cushions beneath them and an umbrella cutting the glare of the sun. Willow's legs weren't in the shade and would hopefully get tanned. Which reminded her, she needed sunscreen.

She reached into her bag and took out a bottle.

Braden's chair was on her left, and he quickly plucked the sunscreen from her hand. "Let me," he said in a gruff voice.

She swung her legs off the edge of the chair, lifted her hair off her back, putting it up in a messy bun with the hair tie on her wrist, giving him a canvas on which to work.

"Tip your head forward," he said.

She did as he asked, and soon his big hands were rubbing the cool lotion into her skin. "Mmm. That feels so good."

"And you smell delicious," he said as his thumbs pressed into her neck.

He continued to massage her back and shoulders, gliding down her arms, coating all the exposed areas he could reach. She relished the feel of his strength and heat as he covered her flesh, rubbing in the cream. "Turn around."

She pivoted, swinging her legs around so they were facing each other. He continued to pour sunscreen onto his hands and work it into her skin, massaging onto her chest, his fingers deliberately dipping beneath her bathing suit, teasing her breasts, coming precariously close to her nipples.

She sucked in a breath, causing him to grin. "Patience," he said. "We're going to enjoy the sunshine first." But as he spoke, he spanned her stomach with his hands, and once again those fingers slid under the fabric, his calloused fingertips rubbing against the top of her pubic bone and pressing inward.

Her eyelids fluttered closed and she moaned, only to have him remove his hands and begin to coat himself with lotion, a sexy grin on his handsome face.

"You're a tease, Braden Prescott." She raised her legs onto the chaise and stretched herself out on the lounge. "I suppose that comes from growing up with a house full of siblings?"

He laughed. "They were all different but yeah. You had to stay on your toes."

She leaned back and closed her eyes but continued the conversation. "I wondered and I hope you don't mind my asking–"

"You can ask me anything," he said.

"How did you feel when you found out Paul Dare and not Jesse Prescott was your biological father?"

Over a year ago, Paul Dare had needed a kidney transplant, making it the right time for him and Braden's mom to tell the Prescott kids the truth. By that time, Willow and Braden had broken up and he'd been gone. She'd heard via Damon that he'd come home when Austin, the match, had donated his kidney. But she hadn't seen or heard from Braden then. Still, she'd wondered how the news had impacted him.

He let out a groan. "Better than you'd think. It's quite a story."

She turned her head and met his gaze. "I want to hear it."

"It's sad actually. My mother and Paul grew up near each other and were best friends. Mom was in love with him and Paul…"

"Is gay. Your poor mom. To love someone she couldn't have."

He nodded. "She took what she could get from him, which was friendship, and he was the best pseudo uncle we could have had. And as for Mom, when they couldn't have kids and it turned out it was because of Jesse, she asked Paul to donate." He shrugged. "I know we should all be mad, but to be honest, it was kind of a relief to know a man I hated and who treated me horribly wasn't my real father. And the guy who was always there? Well, he was my dad."

She smiled. "I'm so glad it wasn't something that broke apart your family."

"If anything, it brought us closer. And it really gave us more insight into Jesse's behavior. He wanted his sons to have the career he couldn't because he was injured and couldn't play, which made him resentful, bitter, and angry. Add to that, he couldn't have children of his own? Yeah, he was a mean son of a bitch."

She reached over and squeezed his hand, sad he'd had to grow up with a man who didn't appreciate his intelligence or kind nature. They hadn't had this kind of deep conversation before, and that was on her. It had been her way of keeping him at a distance, and she was beginning to understand how that made it easier for him to leave her.

She rolled to her side and faced him. "I wish you'd had it easier growing up."

"I feel the same way about you. The difference is I had my mom and my brothers and Bri. I had Uncle Paul and Ron. If you'd had that kind of support…"

He trailed off and she managed a wry smile. "I'd be more open? Giving?"

"More open? Yes. More giving? Not a chance." His kind eyes met hers, their faces close as they lay on their sides on the chairs. "You're one of the most compassionate people I know. You took in Aurora when you barely knew her. You cared enough to come see the health center, and you said you wished you could help. You don't give yourself enough credit."

"Yet *you* do. Even when I've been pretty damned hard on you since you came back?"

"I'm a big boy. I can handle it. Besides, I'm not blameless."

"Let's move on, okay?" She didn't want to get into their past when the present was so good.

Reaching over, he tucked her hair behind her ear. "Sounds good." He stretched his arms up, and his abdominal muscles flexed and she groaned.

"Can we test out the cabana now?"

"Hell yes. If we were completely alone, I'd take you right here, right now." He pushed himself up from his seat and strode over to the far side of her chaise, holding out a hand.

She linked her fingers into his and they disappeared into the cabana. To her surprise, he flipped on overhead lights and released the curtains held back on either side.

"Somehow I think these were meant for cooling off from the sun, not for secret sex," she said, looking at a double-size chaise with a similar plush cushion covered with towels waiting for them.

He let out a low chuckle. "Alex Dare likes to say he sealed the deal with his wife, Madison, in one of these cabanas," he said of Ian's half brother and former professional football player.

She rolled her eyes. "Don't tell me that."

He grinned and walked to her, a predatory gleam in his eyes. "As much as I love that bathing suit, I'd rather see you out of it."

She took his words as a challenge and reached back, unhooking her bikini top, letting it fall to the floor. After kicking off her sandals, her bottoms came next until she stood naked in front of him.

He let out a low growl, removed his trunks, his prominent erection letting her know exactly how much he desired her. She felt the same way, and it was her turn to take control.

She grabbed a towel from a small dresser, dropped it on the floor, and settled to her knees in front of him.

"What are you doing?" he asked.

"What do you think?" Reaching out, she gripped him in her hand, the smooth, velvety feel of him almost as heady as what she planned to do next. Desire pulsed through her, but her focus was on him. She leaned forward and licked the head of his cock, and the salty male taste of him was potent.

He placed a hand on top of her head at the same time she began to pull him deep. Though she wasn't an expert at this by any means, his rough groans told her that her technique was working. He began to rock his hips, thrusting in and out of her mouth, stopping short of hitting the back of her throat. She swallowed around him and his entire body began to shudder.

She grasped his thigh with one hand and slid her other upward until she cupped his balls, massaging them in her palm. He came with a loud shout that she hoped didn't bring others running to see what was going on, and suddenly she was working to swallow as fast and quickly as she could.

She collapsed, catching her breath while he sat down on the lounge with a satisfied groan, leaving her pretty darned pleased with herself, not to mention extremely aroused.

*   *   *

AFTER CATCHING HIS breath, Braden rose and extended a hand, pulling Willow to her feet. "Way to blow my mind." His body still shook with the aftereffects of her talented mouth.

"Among other things," she said with a grin.

He shook his head and laughed. Lying back against the chaise, he crooked a finger her way. No doubt it was her turn, but as much as he wanted to be inside her, he needed recovery time. Which didn't mean he lacked for other ideas to satisfy her.

She started toward him when his cell phone rang from inside the pocket of his swim shorts.

"Ignore it," he said, wanting to grab her, pull her over him, and taste her sweet pussy.

The noise stopped and she began to crawl up to him again. He grabbed her around the waist, and she bent over, her lips coming down on his. He swirled his tongue inside her mouth, drinking her in. He never thought he'd have this chance again, and the fact that she was giving it to him was a fucking miracle.

A moan escaped from her throat, and his dick started to get hard all over again. Looked like he didn't need time after all. He never broke the kiss, moving his hands upward and cupping her breasts and pinching her stiff nipples between his fingers. She rolled her hips over his cock and suddenly sat up.

"I need you inside me." Lifting her body, she grasped his erection in her hands, settled her wet sex over the head of his dick, and slid down on a moan, her slick walls clasping him in tight heat.

At the snug feel, his eyes shut tight and he thrust up to meet her. "Fuck, you feel good."

"I'm going to make you feel even better," she said and began to slide up and down his now rock-hard shaft.

He grasped her hips and helped her rise and fall, slamming down hard, hips rolling forward each time their bodies met. All he felt was her.

All he cared about was making her come. For him.

Beneath him. With him. Reaching out, he slid his finger over her clit, pressing down and moving in deliberate circles that she began to imitate with the motion of her hips.

"Braden, Braden, Braden!" The sound of his name on her lips was everything.

She tilted her head back, arching her body and seeking more pressure that he was only too happy to give.

He gritted his teeth, holding back, refusing to give in to his orgasm until she'd had hers. Instead he took her in, hair falling down her back, her gorgeous curves riding him, when suddenly her sex clamped tight around him as she fell over the edge. Her climax hit and it was the most gorgeous sight.

He waited until she'd ridden out her pleasure, only then letting himself go. He thrust up again and again, but it didn't take long for him to find release, losing himself inside her completely.

She collapsed on top of him, and he slipped out of her, totally spent. She snuggled against him, and he gathered her in his arms, her head on his shoulder, and they lay in silence, both catching their breath, until the sound of laughter reminded him of where they were.

"We should get dressed in case someone comes by," she said, stepping around the chaise and bending to pick up the pieces of her bikini.

They'd gotten carried away in here, but he didn't regret it for a second. Nodding, he rose to his feet, cleaned up with a towel while she did the same, and they put on their clothes.

A few minutes later, he grasped her hand and they walked out of the cabana to find a couple had settled on chairs nearby.

"Jesus, buddy, next time take it to your room."

Willow pulled him faster toward their chairs while Braden merely gave the guy a thumbs-up. What else could he do? he thought wryly.

As he reached his chair and sat down, he felt his phone in his pocket, remembered it had rung earlier, and reached for his cell, saw Austin had called, and narrowed his gaze.

Willow settled in beside him and glanced over. "Anything important?"

He clicked over to the messages and read the transcription. "It's Austin. Evie verified the Kingstons. They are Aurora's family."

Eyes wide, Willow blew out a long breath. "Okay then. We tell her and she can meet the one who's in town. Lincoln? Was that his name?"

Braden nodded.

Willow bent her knees and leaned her head back on the cushion. "I'm worried," she admitted. "Or maybe I'm scared. I don't know these people, but the best thing for her is if they accept her with open arms."

"And she ends up leaving with them." He finished her thought for her.

She nodded, her entire demeanor withdrawn.

Not from him, necessarily, but from life, which she anticipated throwing her another hit. He would have liked to extend their afternoon, but with one glance at Willow's concerned face, their fun day came to an abrupt end.

"Do you want to go back to your place and talk to Aurora? Or would you rather head over to Dare Nation and pull her from work to break the news?" he asked.

Willow sighed. "We're not dressed to walk into an office, so why don't you take me home, and you can go back to your place. We can shower, change, and you can come by tonight and we'll break the news to Aurora once she's had time to unwind after work?"

He nodded. "Sure thing." Knowing this was difficult for Willow to deal with, he wanted to handle things on her terms.

As they gathered their things together, he couldn't help the disappointment he felt at having their day cut short. Still, he'd had her in his arms and he'd been inside her body. He couldn't exactly complain.

"Braden?" He'd been lost in thought, and he

shook his head, then met her gaze. "Yeah. Sorry. What's up?"

She treated him to a soft smile he wanted to kiss. "Thank you for today."

"You're welcome. I enjoyed it a lot, and we can definitely do it again soon."

A flash of hope flickered in her eyes. "I hope so."

He winked at her. "Count on it."

Chapter Eleven

WILLOW SAT BESIDE Aurora with Braden across from them as they explained the fact that she had family she didn't know about who wanted to meet her.

The young girl, who'd come home from work, showered, and changed into a pair of maternity pajamas, turned to Willow in shock. "I don't understand. I have a brother from New York who's here in Florida?"

Willow reached for her trembling hand. "You have an entire family, although Lincoln is the one who flew here to meet you. It's exciting news!"

"I have family?" she asked again. "How? My mother left me, said she didn't know who my father was, and Grandma didn't know, either."

Willow shot Braden an imploring glance. She needed help explaining the complicated story.

He leaned forward, hands on his thighs. "Your mother had an affair with a married man, and he didn't want his wife to know about it. When she got pregnant, he ... paid her to take care of you, which she obviously didn't do. He died recently and his son found the monthly checks cashed from his account." Braden cleared his throat and hesitated with the rest.

Willow knew it wasn't easy for him to break the hardest news, so she took over. "They hired a private investigator and found your mom," Willow said gently. "She's been living off the money, but she admitted to leaving you with her mother." And not taking Aurora in after the older woman passed away. There was no reason to state the obvious and hurt the young woman more.

Aurora sniffed, her eyes filled with tears. "My mom. She's alive and fine? And living off money meant to help her with me?"

"I'm sorry, sweetheart. But as soon as Lincoln and his siblings found out they had a half sister, he flew here to meet you and"—Willow drew a deep breath— "bring you back with him. They want to get to know you and take care of you."

She dipped her head, her tears flowing now, her hands on her belly. No doubt Aurora's story had highs and lows, Willow thought. A mother who'd abandoned her and basically stolen money that should have gone for her care, but in the end, Aurora was gaining a family. And wasn't that every foster child's dream? Even when they grew up, deep down, everyone had a need to be loved and wanted.

"Are you okay?" Willow asked.

Looking up, Aurora nodded. "When can I meet him? And I don't want to go alone."

"Don't worry. You won't," Willow said, looking to Braden.

"There's a game Sunday and we took off today. What if—"

"Can you call him now?" Aurora asked, cutting him off, her enthusiasm obviously growing.

"Umm…" Braden appeared unsure.

"Of course," Willow said, certain Braden's hesitancy was out of concern, but given Aurora's reaction, the sooner the better. Willow didn't want her to have to spend the night obsessing and worrying when they could arrange for her to meet her brother now.

"Sure." Braden rose to his feet. "Evie left me the number. Let me step outside to make the call and I'll be right back."

Willow had no doubt Braden walked out so he could also let Lincoln know his sister was eight months pregnant so his shock wouldn't show when he walked in tonight.

"Oh my God," Aurora said as soon as he left the apartment. "I need to pull myself together. I need to change into clothes! And put on some makeup so I don't scare him to death." She rose and dashed for the bedroom, leaving Willow to stare after her with a grin on her face.

Braden walked back in, his expression also a happy one. "He'll be here in thirty minutes. Where's Aurora?" he asked, looking around.

"Getting ready to meet her brother. Did you tell him she's pregnant?" Willow asked more quietly.

He nodded. "He took it in stride. And just a warning, he sounds like a man used to getting his way. He's a lot like Ian in that way. In fact, I think Lincoln is already making plans in his head to bring Aurora back with him as soon as possible," he warned her. Braden clasped her hands in his. "Are you going to be okay with that?"

Willow tilted her head toward the bathroom, where the noise of the blow dryer sounded. "If it means she's happy and has a support system? Absolutely." Although she'd miss Aurora's presence, she couldn't deny her happiness made Willow ecstatic.

"You do realize we didn't tell her she's related to a rock star and a famous actor?" he asked.

Willow shrugged. "Something tells me it's just going to be icing on the cake. And here I was worried about how she'd take the news," she said wryly. "Of course, it probably hasn't sunk in yet about her mother."

"Or she's already come to terms with not having a mother in her life, and the fact that she was abandoned already told her all she needed to know about the woman who gave birth to her."

Willow nodded. "That I can relate to, and it makes sense to me. I hope she never goes looking for the woman, because the only thing down that path is heartache."

He pulled her into his arms, and she sighed, leaning her head against his chest. "Regardless, she's excited and that's what matters."

"Agreed."

Not long after Aurora finally finished getting dressed and made up, she joined them in the living room, looking the best Willow had ever seen her. In the very short time she'd been working for Dare Nation, she'd blossomed into a pretty young woman wearing makeup, clean clothing that fit, and a light in her eyes she hadn't had when Willow met her that day in the diner. Tonight the glow was even more prominent.

As were her nerves. Lincoln Kingston had better be a good, decent man, Willow thought, glancing at the poor girl pacing the room. If the doorbell didn't ring soon, there'd be a hole in the carpet.

"What if he judges me for being pregnant and not knowing who the father is?"

"He won't," Willow assured her. Braden had vetted him damned carefully on that. He'd promised while they waited for the young woman to get ready.

"You mentioned they're wealthy?" A conversation Willow had had with her when she'd gone in to check on her only to find four outfits on the bed.

She'd helped Aurora pick one while giving her information about her new family. Select information. If she'd told her about Dash Kingston, the rock star, and Xander Kingston, the actor, Aurora's freak out would be even worse.

"You've been around Braden's brothers, and they all have money. Not to mention the athletes who come into Dare Nation. You'll be fine," Willow continued to reassure her.

She met Braden's amused smile and shook her head. It wouldn't help for either of them to make light of such an important situation, but the truth was Aurora's reactions were so sweet.

When the ring sounded, all three of them startled, despite being ready for their guest's arrival. Aurora smoothed her hand over her belly, her pretty blue top matching her eyes.

"Ready?" Braden asked and she nodded.

He opened the door, and an extremely handsome man stood on the threshold, wearing a pair of dark jeans and a pale blue collared short-sleeve Polo shirt. His dark hair was perfectly and expensively cut, and an air of self-assurance surrounded him. If she hadn't been so far gone for Braden, she'd definitely be attracted. After all, she wasn't dead and her hormones reacted.

But the most striking thing about him, at least for Willow, was his blue eyes that were so like Aurora's and the similarity in their facial features. Defined but full lips, a perfectly straight nose, and a strong jaw on him, less so on her. They certainly were related.

"Lincoln Kingston?" Braden asked.

The man who was as tall and broad as Braden nodded. "Braden Prescott?"

With a nod, Braden extended his hand, and the men engaged in a power handshake that was obvious even from a distance.

"Call me Linc," he said.

"Come on in, Linc." Braden stepped aside, and the other man entered, his intent gaze zeroing in on Aurora.

"This is Willow James, my – the woman Aurora's been living with recently." Braden gestured to Willow and she gave him a smile and a wave.

He nodded, appreciation in his gaze. "A pleasure to meet you."

"And this is your sister, Aurora Michaels."

Aurora stared at Linc wide-eyed, a mixture of awe and fear of rejection in her eyes and expression.

Willow held her breath as Linc strode over, and

though she expected this stern man to extend a hand to Aurora for a shake, he placed his hand beneath her chin. "You have our eyes," he said and pulled her into his arms for an embrace.

A lump rose to Willow's throat. Because she had experienced the loneliness and fear of being an unwanted foster through the age of sixteen, she literally felt Aurora's initial panic and now the complete release of emotion as she received Linc's unconditional acceptance. So much so that Willow's own knees nearly buckled.

As if sensing her empathetic response and unspoken need, Braden was there, bracing her with a strong arm around her waist and all of his support.

Once the emotional greeting was complete, they all settled in Willow's small living room, making the best of her sofa and one club chair.

Before Linc could speak, Aurora began peppering him with questions. "How many brothers and sisters do you have? I mean do I have? Are they all in New York? What does everyone do?"

Linc's eyes crinkled with warmth and amusement as he replied. "I'm the oldest and I run the family company. I'm sure you'll learn a lot more if you decide to come work with me."

"Me?" she said on a squeak. "But I don't have a college degree! I barely graduated high school. And I just started learning office work at Dare Nation. Plus I live in Florida."

Linc raised an eyebrow at that, and Willow could all but read his thoughts. *For now. You live in Florida for now.*

"Why don't you let me tell you some more about the family since I have the distinct feeling you're missing key information?" He shot both Willow and Braden a glance.

Braden shrugged. "I didn't want to freak her out all at once."

"What's going on?" Aurora asked.

Linc's low chuckle had her opening her eyes wide. "Our brother, Xander, is an–"

"Xander Kingston. The actor!" Aurora nearly yelled. "No way!"

"Yes way." He grinned. "And Dash is a rock star."

At this point the poor girl's eyes were about to pop out of her head.

"And Chloe is our sister."

Aurora blinked, tears in her eyes. "I have a sister," she whispered, that fact impacting her more than her famous siblings. "How is this my life?"

Linc's smile was grim. "It should have been your life sooner. I'm sorry for what my father did, but the minute I found out about you, I began looking. I just couldn't find you until you took a legitimate job that gave me a lead."

She shook her head. "I don't understand why you care? I'm an illegitimate child of a man who didn't want me. Aren't you embarrassed by my very existence?"

His wince was at once protective and sad, Willow thought.

"I think you'll find we Kingston kids are very resilient and we protect our own. I'm glad you've had support lately, but do you have plans for once the baby is born?"

Willow leaned into Braden as Aurora answered.

"No," she whispered. "I don't have health insurance yet, although Bri said she's submitted the papers. And I didn't know what I'd do about work and someone to watch the baby. I don't have my own apartment. I'm staying here and Willow's been sleeping on the sofa. I can't bring a baby home with me because it's just not fair to her—"

Willow felt the heat of Linc's surprised but grateful stare. "Aurora, you can stay until you figure something out. I told you that." She wanted the young woman to know she had choices.

Aurora's damp gaze met hers. "And I appreciate that but we both know it can't really work. And I can't afford my own place…" She was starting to get worked up, and Willow jumped up from her seat.

She walked over to Aurora, who'd taken the chair, and put a hand on her shoulder. "Shh. Calm down, please. Getting upset isn't good for you or the baby."

"Can I get a word in?" Linc asked.

All eyes turned his way.

"We have a variety of solutions in New York. The family estate where my father used to live still has staff that are loyal to our family, and they were always good to us growing up. We own apartment buildings around Manhattan. Each of us has a trust fund, and I'm working on getting yours set up to atone for how you grew up and everything you've lacked your entire life."

By now Aurora was crying in earnest. Not because she was sad but for the simple reason that she was overwhelmed, Willow knew.

"Can you give her time to process?" Braden asked. "As much as everything you're offering is the answer to her prayers, she needs to adjust to her new reality."

Linc scowled, obviously used to getting his way.

Undeterred, Braden continued. "I realize you have her best interest at heart, but the few emotional connections she has are here."

Willow wanted to wrap her arms around his neck and kiss him for standing up for Aurora's needs and not letting Linc, despite his good intentions, take over her life.

With reluctance, the man nodded. "I could help

you find an apartment, a nanny, and get set up here, if that's what you decide," he said to Aurora. "But I also hope you realize your family wants to get to know you. We would like you to be a part of our lives, and I'd rather take you home with me."

Aurora pressed her hand against her forehead. "This is so much so soon. Braden's right. I need to think. And to get to know you more."

"How much longer can you fly? In your pregnancy, I mean?" Linc asked Aurora.

She lifted her head and shrugged her shoulders. "I never asked. There was no reason to."

"Up to thirty-six weeks," Braden said. "I've been her doctor, in case you didn't run your own checks on the people in her life."

"Of course I did," Linc muttered.

Braden smirked, obviously having guessed right. "She has two weeks before I'd prefer she didn't get on an airplane."

Linc drew a deep breath and nodded. "I'll stay for a week. We'll get to know one another and then you can make a decision. Fair?" he asked, but it was clear he intended to sway her to return home with him.

"Yes. Thank you," Aurora said. "I'd like that."

"Now that that's settled, why don't you two make plans for the week, and then I'd say Aurora and the baby need some rest." Braden's voice brooked no argument. He wasn't about to let Linc roll over him, and Willow admired him for standing up to this commanding presence.

Braden rose from his seat. "If you two would like to come to the Thunder football game on Sunday, I can get you box seats," he offered.

Linc had stood as well. "That sounds fun. Would you like to go?" he asked Aurora.

She nodded.

Willow thought it would be a good ice breaker to talk while watching the game.

"Willow, walk me out? It'll give them time to make plans," Braden said.

"Thanks," Aurora said to them both, her eyes gleaming with nervous energy.

Braden smiled at her and Willow nodded. "I'll be back in a few minutes," she said.

She accompanied him to the catwalk, shutting the door behind them. The humidity and heat hit her immediately. "That went better than expected."

He nodded. "But Lincoln Kingston is a man used to getting what he wants."

"But in this case, I think it's in Aurora's best interest to go with him," she said sadly. "I'll miss her, but to find a family this late in life? And one who doesn't resent how she became one of them? Who would want to deny her that?"

He placed his hands on her hips and pulled her close. "It's not like you're losing her for good. You can visit any time and vice versa."

She breathed him in, taking in his solid masculine scent. "I'm glad you're here." When Aurora left, she'd be alone again in her apartment, and while a part of her wouldn't mind the privacy and her bed back, a larger part would miss the young girl.

"I'm not going anywhere," he said, tipping her head upward and placing his lips on hers, his tongue sweeping through her mouth.

She kissed him back, her heart pounding in her chest, hoping he meant it. He was slowly regaining her trust, but her heart couldn't handle the pain if he left her again.

*   *   *

BRADEN STOOD ON the sidelines of the Thunder game on Sunday. Fourth quarter with five minutes left to play, one time-out remaining for the Thunder, two for the opposing team. For Florida, the day had a light feel, less humidity than they'd had lately, and he appreciated that fact as the sun baked down overhead. He adjusted the brim of his cap and watched the play unfold on the field. Milling around were the doctors assigned to today's game. Unfortunately that group included Cole Walsh, because despite the fact that

Braden despised the man, he couldn't prevent him from doing his job unless he had a valid reason.

And he wished the man's watching Willow bend over one of their rookie players was on the list of justifiable grounds. Only he had the right to ogle his girl.

"Walsh!" Braden all but barked at him. "Go check out Reilly's ankle!"

Cole scowled at him but did as he'd ordered, enabling Braden to turn his gaze back to Willow for a brief moment.

Her hair had been braided and hung down her back, and just watching her filled him with a sense of satisfaction and pleasure. They were finally on a solid path, and he had every intention of keeping them there.

A whistle blew and the defense ran off the field. Damon and the offense took their place. Damon called out the play and darted left. Just as he threw the ball, the defensive end from the other team slammed into him, tackling him and taking him down, the sound causing Braden's stomach to churn.

Panic hit as it always did when one of his brothers was injured, and Braden held his breath as he waited for the men to separate and stand on their own. Except when the defensive end rose to his feet, Damon remained still on the field.

He glanced at Coach Carson, got the nod, and with the other doctors on scene, ran onto the field where his brother lay motionless. Everything happened in a rushed blur of protocol and suppressing his emotions.

"He hit his head on the ground," Coach said from behind them.

Another possible concussion, Braden thought. Fuck. His brother had just recently recovered from one blow to the head. He had a history of concussions in high school. If he did have another one, he was increasing his chances of permanent damage. Braden refused to think about CTE, brain degeneration caused by repeated head traumas. Right now he had to deal with this injury. Thank God he was breathing on his own.

Willow arrived in the next instant and took over her job, immobilizing his neck and removing his face mask and shoulder pads, just as Damon regained consciousness, blinking, wincing, and immediately attempting to move, but those around him held him down.

"Damon, stay still," Braden said. "Can you tell me where you are?"

"On the field. At the stadium. What happened?"

Dr. Stadtler, the concussion specialist, stepped in and talked to Damon, slowly helping him to his feet, at which point the crowd in the stands erupted in cheer.

He walked off the field, and the doctor in charge now immediately sat him down and performed a concussion test, comparing his time to the test he'd taken pregame. It wasn't good. Damon's response was slower and he was obviously dizzy and nauseous.

"He's out." Stadtler made the call and Damon began to argue.

Willow came up behind him. "What's going on?"

"Failed the CPT."

"Shit." She slipped her hand into his and squeezed once, letting him know she was there for him, before stepping back to maintain professional distance.

Despite the fact that Damon was his brother, Braden did his job, remaining on the field while Damon went to the hospital for X-rays, a CAT scan, and a routine medical checkup. Everyone took head injuries seriously, and this one looked like it was going to be a problem.

* * *

IT WASN'T UNTIL the game ended and Braden made sure the injuries were cared for that he left to be with his brother, and though Willow wanted desperately to be there for them both, she couldn't get to the hospital for hours after the game. She had a job to do, and she stayed with her players to make sure they had everything they needed after a rough four-plus hours that left them bruised and beaten up, as usual. They'd lost in the last five minutes, Damon's injury on everyone's mind, which put the guys in horrible moods.

Finally, she made her way to her car and drove to the hospital, her team badge allowing her past the main waiting room. She wasn't surprised to find the Prescott family gathered in a smaller room without other visitors.

Christine stood, shoulders back but worry on her face, Bri standing by her side. Jaxon and Macy, along with Austin and Quinn, sat in chairs near each other, talking low. All looked up and treated her to a wave or a smile.

"I'm sorry if I'm interrupting," she said.

"No!" Christine Prescott stepped over to her. "I appreciate you coming."

"Have you heard anything yet?" Willow asked.

Christine, wearing Damon's jersey number, shook her head with a grim but stoic smile. "Braden and Evie are in with him. I'm sure one of them will know something soon and come tell us."

She was the mother of three professional athletes. No doubt she'd been through her share of injuries with them before, and Willow admired her strength and wished she'd had a parent who'd drop everything and show up if she were hurt. Siblings, too. Another reason for Aurora, who'd been bonding with Linc these past few days, to leave with him when their week was up.

"Would you like me to go see what I can find out? I can pull the *I'm a team trainer* card and see if they'll let me back." Willow wanted to give them all good news and ease the pain on their faces.

"Would you?" Christine asked.

"That would be great," Bri said, her arm around her mother's shoulders.

Willow nodded. "Listen. He was conscious when they brought him in. That's always a good sign."

Christine nodded gratefully, and Willow excused herself to check on Damon and find Braden.

Chapter Twelve

B RADEN SAT BESIDE Damon's bedside in a chair, Evie on the edge of the mattress. The doctor had come in and explained he had a severe concussion. *Again.* That he had a sufficient history of head injuries to warrant suggesting he not continue to play or risk permanent brain damage in the future.

After he'd dropped that bomb, the three of them sat in silence, Braden offering to leave but Evie and Damon asking him to stay.

The moments ticked by and Braden broke the silence. "You don't have to make a decision right this minute. You can't play for a while anyway." Although if he had his way, Damon would retire and enter Dare Nation, the closest thing they had to a family business, in any capacity he chose. No doubt Austin would be the first to extend an offer when he heard the news.

"There's really no choice to make. I have a wife who's pregnant." He lifted Evie's hand to his mouth and kissed her. "I want to be there to raise my kids, not let my brain turn to mush and lose the rest of my life because I chose playing over my family."

Evie sniffled and tears dripped down her cheeks. "I'm so sorry, Damon. But I can't deny how glad I am you're choosing us."

"I'll deal, you know? It won't be easy to leave it behind, but I'll figure out a new path." He winked at his wife.

"Alex Dare has programs that help players who have to retire early, but I think you're going to be just fine. Think about your path and talk to Austin. Or Ian about a front-office job." Braden pushed himself to his feet. "Okay if I give the family the news?"

Damon rested his head back against the pillows. "Yeah. And send them home. I promise I'll be in touch. Right now I just want to talk to Evie, okay?"

Braden nodded. "I'll try but you know they're going to want to see for themselves that you're okay. Call me if you need me," he said more to Evie than to his brother because Damon would never admit to weakness.

He walked out of the darkened room, where no lights were on because it hurt Damon's eyes, and nearly bumped into Willow. He was so grateful to see her, he opened his arms and she walked right into them.

"God, I'm glad to see you."

She tipped her head back and smiled. "Rough day. How's Damon?"

He filled her in and she sighed. "That's awful. He's so talented and is such a presence and idol for the younger players on the team."

"I know but I give him credit for doing what's best for himself and his family. Still, I don't think Ian's going to be happy, though he will support Damon's decision."

"Do you think he'll go to work with Austin at Dare Nation?" she asked.

He shrugged, unsure what his brother would do. "Time will tell, right?"

She nodded. "I promised your mom I'd see if I could find out what's going on."

He took her hand, squeezing tight. "Let's do it together."

As they headed back to the small room where Braden's family waited, his cell buzzed in his pocket. He pulled it out, glanced at the number, and declined the call.

"Anything important?" she asked.

"Nothing that can't wait." He shoved his phone back into his pocket, and together they went to talk to his family.

His mother had cried, not because she cared what her sons did for their careers but for the disappointment she knew Damon must be feeling. Austin had gone into big brother/agent mode and had immediately begun plotting alternative jobs for his sibling, starting and ending with Dare Nation if Austin had his way. Everyone else grew silent and sad, digesting the information and probably figuring out what they'd say to Damon when they saw him.

Despite Damon wanting to be alone, his mom had gone back to see her son and everyone else would file in and out over the next hour, so Braden had no problem deciding it was time to go home. Today had been a long fucking day, and Braden wanted nothing more than to climb into bed and crash, but he didn't want to do it alone.

When he'd looked up and seen Willow coming toward him, the weight on his shoulders had lifted. Having her by his side when they'd broken Damon's career-ending news to his family had given him the strength to deal with everyone's myriad reactions.

He glanced at her, leaning against the wall, looking as beat as he felt.

"Ready to leave?" he asked.

She nodded then yawned, covering her mouth with her hand. "Excuse me," she said. "I'm just wiped out."

"Me, too. Let's go." He grasped her hand, called into the room that they were leaving, and led her out.

They wound their way through the hospital corridors and out to the parking lot in tired silence.

"My car is over there," she said, pointing to the

opposite side of the lot from where Braden had left his vehicle.

He changed directions and walked her over, pausing when she reached her door and unlocked it with her key fob.

"Stay at my place tonight?" he asked, needing to fall asleep with her in his arms.

She glanced up at him and wrinkled her nose, her expression torn. "We have to work tomorrow and I don't have clothes."

"I promise we'll be up in time for you to go home, shower, and change." If he had his way, she would start leaving clothes at his house, but tonight wasn't the time to get into a serious conversation. "I need you," he admitted though it wasn't easy.

Until now he'd kept things light, but after the day he'd had, the fear for his unconscious brother, he wasn't above taking things deeper.

She stroked his cheek with her fingertips, her gaze meeting his. "I'll follow you home, okay? Just let me text Aurora and tell her not to expect me tonight."

"Sounds good," he said, relieved.

A short while later, they were in his bedroom. He'd given her a tee shirt, and she excused herself to take a quick shower, and once she finished, he did the same. They were both drained, and he didn't press for a joint shower because, despite how much he desired her, he lacked the mental energy and stamina to do more than hold her as they fell asleep.

And when they finally crawled into his bed, he wrapped his body around hers, feeling at peace with her in his arms.

*   *   *

THE NEXT MORNING, Willow woke before Braden and prior to the alarm he'd set, his warm body curled around hers. The sound of his heavy breathing told her he was in a deep sleep. Knowing how exhausted he'd been last night, both physically and emotionally, she let him be, quietly sliding out from beneath his arm that lay over her.

When he'd admitted to needing her yesterday, he'd slipped past the final barrier she'd kept in place, and she'd melted inside. It meant something, knowing she could give to him as much as he'd been doing for her. She couldn't fight herself or him any longer, and she was done trying. She'd gone and fallen in love with him, fully and completely, this time without any more hesitation or reservation. She just needed him not to disappoint her.

Leaving him a quick note that said she'd see him at work, she went home to change, eat something, and head over to the stadium.

When she arrived home, she let herself inside and

discovered Aurora at the small kitchen table, drinking a cup of tea.

"Morning," Willow said, dropping her keys into the basket where she kept them.

"Morning."

"What are you doing up so early?" she asked.

Aurora shrugged. "I couldn't sleep. Plus I wanted to talk to you before you left for work."

Willow sat down in a chair beside her. "Sure. What's up?"

Aurora twirled a strand of her hair around her finger and found it hard to look Willow in the eye.

"Hey. Talk to me. Whatever it is, I promise it's fine," Willow said.

She drew a deep breath. "I've really liked getting to know Linc and Jordan, Linc's personal assistant and best friend."

"Hey, that's great!" Willow said, meaning it.

Aurora glanced up. "You've been so good to me. You and Braden both but–"

"You're going to New York to meet your family and let them take care of you."

Aurora nodded, tears in her eyes. "Are you angry?"

"Oh my gosh, no! I'm so very happy for you," Willow said, grasping the young girl's hand. "What is it we both wanted growing up? People to love us? You have that now. And you'll still have me. I promise I'm not going anywhere. We can talk, FaceTime, and I can come visit. I'm going to want to see the baby!"

Willow said everything she could to make it easier for Aurora to go. To be at peace with her choice. And to know she'd still have Willow here if she needed her.

"Yeah?" Aurora's face lit up. "I'd love that!" She grinned. "Did you know Linc has a private jet? We're going to fly to New York on it tomorrow."

So soon. Willow's stomach twisted in sadness, but at the same time, she couldn't help but laugh at Aurora's enthusiasm. "That's really cool. Can we have a final dinner together tonight?"

Aurora nodded. "Definitely."

Willow smiled. "Okay, I have to grab clothes and get dressed for work, but tonight you're mine." She started for the bedroom when Aurora spoke.

"Don't forget to invite Braden!" she called out.

Willow was very happy to do just that.

* * *

BRADEN SAT IN the office at Thunder Stadium, trying to concentrate when his mind was on both his brother and the woman who'd slipped out of his bed early this morning. She'd had to rush home in order to get ready for work, but she'd left him a note. As he'd lain in bed, the scent of her lingering on his sheets, he couldn't help but think about how perfect they fit together, how well their lives meshed, and wondered whether it was time to tell her how he felt about her.

A knock sounded on his door, interrupting his thoughts, which he didn't mind since he hadn't come to a decision yet anyway. "Come in!"

Hudson walked in, shut the door behind him, and sat down in a chair, making himself comfortable. "How's Damon?"

"I spoke to him this morning. Usual concussion symptoms and taking it easy. Evie's making sure he doesn't move from their bed."

Braden was worried about his retirement, the decision he'd made so easily, and the announcement, but even this morning, Damon insisted he'd accepted his fate and was at peace with it. Since meeting Evie, his priorities had changed, something Braden could now understand.

"Give him my best," Hudson said. "Now we need to talk about the clinic."

Braden nodded. "I agree. The place needs an infusion of cash, and I've been thinking about how to come up with the funds."

"Same. You want to buy the place, don't you?" He knew what his friend was thinking, because he'd been considering the same thing.

"What I want and what I can afford to do are very different." Hudson scowled. "My grandfather left me a trust fund, but my father is trustee. There is no way that son of a bitch is going to give me the funding."

Braden rested his hands on the desk. "You won't know unless you try. I'll have to go to my uncle Paul for a loan."

Hudson's mouth lifted in a smirk. "Somehow I think the man who's really your father and has your brother's kidney inside him isn't going to say no."

That made Braden laugh. "Probably not. Besides, he'll see the merit in helping people who need it. We can turn the place into a one-stop health center with new equipment and qualified professionals who care."

"Here's hoping my father sees the same value. It's all about money to him." Hudson paused in thought. "This is something I'm going to have to do in person, though," he said with a definite pissed-off tone and scowl. "Ever since Evan died, he's been after me to give up medicine to come home and join the family business."

Braden leaned forward on his desk. He knew it'd been rough on Hudson since his older brother had passed away. They hadn't been close, because like his father, Evan's only focus had been the family business, but Hudson missed his sibling. And when Evan had been alive, Hudson's dad had relied on him for carrying on the family legacy, from the business to providing an heir. His parent was old-fashioned in every way. After Evan's sudden and unexpected aneurysm, the pressure on Hudson had been heavy and ongoing. Which was why he'd refused to return to New York after their MSF stint.

"I don't envy you," Braden said. "We can apply to the bank for a loan?"

Hudson nodded. "We may have to but let me try my father first. The money's mine. Maybe he'll see reason."

"Sounds good. You know I have your back."

He slid his foot to the floor and rose from his seat. "I appreciate that."

"Hello?" Bri walked in without announcing her presence and Braden rolled his eyes.

"Ever hear of knocking?" he asked.

"Not when it comes to you. I had to meet with a client, and I was hoping I could grab you for lunch?" Her gaze slid to Hudson, and if Braden wasn't mistaken, he saw a flash of interest in his sister's gaze.

Braden and Hudson hadn't talked much about his past relationships or what he wanted for the future beyond not letting his father dictate his life or his choices. If Bri was interested, Hudson better not hurt her.

"Hello, Brianne." Hudson turned toward her, and a smile lifted his sister's lips.

"Hey, Hudson. Want to join us?" she asked.

Braden laughed at her assumption that lunch was definite. "I haven't said yes yet."

She leaned against the doorframe, professional in her slacks and blouse, her dark hair like Braden's pulled into a sleek ponytail. "But you will because you miss me," she said, sure of herself and him.

And she was right. "Fine, lunch it is. Hudson? You in?" Braden asked.

"Wish I could but I have a patient scheduled who could take a while." Regret etched his features as he glanced at Bri. "I've got to get going. Good to see you," he said to her before looking over at Braden. "I'll keep you posted."

Braden nodded, and with a wave, Hudson left them alone. Bri walked farther inside, leaving the door still partially ajar.

"So where do you want to eat?" she asked, wrinkling her nose in thought. "How's the deli you love?"

His stomach growled at the idea of a huge sandwich with a variety of meats, cole slaw, and French fries.

"I'll take that as a yes," Bri said, laughing.

"Knock knock!" a male voice called out.

"What is this place today? Grand Central Station? Come in," Braden said, and a familiar face stepped into the room.

"Adam!" Braden was shocked to see his Doctors

Without Borders colleague who, the last time he'd spoken to him, had still been in Brazil.

Bri glanced at the other man, curiosity in her gaze.

"Bri, this is Adam Niles. We worked together the last two years. Adam, my twin sister, Bri." Braden gestured between them.

"It's so nice to meet you," Bri said, shaking Adam's hand.

"Same here." Adam smiled at her.

"Listen, I can kill some time before lunch so you two can catch up," his sister said, rightly realizing he and Adam needed time alone. "I'll see you later." She turned to Adam and smiled before walking out.

"Come on in and sit down! What are you doing here?" Braden gestured for his friend to sit while he leaned against his desk.

Adam, tanned from working in the sun, wore a pair of khaki pants and a short-sleeved shirt. His sandy-blond hair was long, as usual, but he'd cleaned up his beard to a short scruff.

He leaned one arm over the back of his chair. "I came to say hello … and to try and convince you to return with me. I can't tell you how short-staffed we are and how much we miss you and Hudson."

He shook his head. "Not happening," he said, without needing time to think. "My family and my life are here." Not to mention Willow was, as well. And if there was any reason to stay put, she was it.

"Come on. You loved your time with us," Adam said, his tone imploring.

"I did. And I learned a lot about myself while I was with MSF. But it's not my life's calling. I found other ways to give of myself right here."

"Treating athletes who earn hundreds of thousands of dollars a year?" Adam asked skeptically. The man always had a chip on his shoulder about the wealthy. It had taken Braden and Hudson time to win him over and gain his trust, to prove they weren't rich boys running away from home but men looking to make a difference.

Still, Braden stiffened, straightening his shoulders. "I'll have you know these men work damned hard, but that's not what I'm talking about."

He went on to explain about the downtown clinic and his and Hudson's dream for the place, effectively ending Adam's hope that if he couldn't convince Braden, maybe Hudson would want to return. Though Braden promised to relay the offer to Hudson so the man could make his own decision, they both knew the answer.

Thirty minutes later, Adam had accepted defeat gracefully. "Well, it was worth a try. I'll continue my recruiting elsewhere," he said, resigned. He rose to his feet.

Braden walked over and slapped him on the back. "I wish you the best." He walked him to the door, figuring he'd go see if Willow wanted to join him and Bri for lunch before grabbing his sister and heading to the deli. He'd fill them both in on his talk with Hudson and their desire to improve the health care center. Bri would use her PR brain to find a way to gain donations, he was sure, and he could use her help.

Braden stepped out the door and into the hall first, immediately bumping into Cole. "What the fuck are you doing hanging around outside my door?" He really needed to talk to Ian about letting this asshole go.

Cole eyed him warily. "I came to talk to you, to see how Damon was doing, but I realized you were busy with someone."

Braden moved aside so Adam could leave the office and the other man left with a brief wave.

As for Cole, Braden couldn't exactly get pissed at him for wanting to check on the team's star player. They hadn't made his decision to retire public yet nor would they spread the word around the staff.

"He's as well as he can be with a severe concussion," Braden said.

"Well, wish him my best." Cole turned and walked away, leaving Braden to shake his head at the man. Whatever had Willow seen in the guy?

Speaking of Willow, he pivoted and headed toward

the training room, but when he saw her deeply involved with one of their linebackers, he knew she wouldn't be able to make lunch. He'd just bring something back for her since she had a tendency to skip the meal in favor of work. The protein bar she ate instead didn't fill her, leaving her starving for dinner.

He shook his head and went to find his sister.

* * *

WILLOW FINISHED UP with Leon James, who had a high ankle sprain and wanted to play this Sunday when they both knew he couldn't return yet. His frustration was palpable, but no matter how much work she did with him, time was his best friend. Not that he wanted to hear it.

She washed her hands at the scrub sink in the main area, hoping she had a few minutes to grab lunch before her next patient.

"Hi," a voice said from way too close.

She jumped in surprise, spun, and came face-to-face with Cole. Her heart pounded too hard in her chest, and despite the fact that she was in a room with other trainers and therapists spread around various tables, her nerves screamed inside her.

She backed away, hitting the sink behind her. "Cole. What do you want?" She breathed in but he was still too close, and the scent of his cologne made her sick. "And could you please get out of my personal space?"

When he didn't move fast enough, she ducked to the side and escaped his cloying presence.

"Willow."

Closing her eyes briefly, she turned. "What?"

"You should call off your guard dog. He threatened me the other day, you know?"

No, she didn't know. "No doubt you deserved it. You're starting to freak me out. What is wrong with you?"

He narrowed his gaze. "I've told you before, I'm just looking out for you. And on that note, did you know your new boyfriend had a visit from a colleague from Doctors Without Borders?"

She swallowed hard, but she wasn't going to let Cole see her worry. Just because Braden had met with a friend from his traveling days didn't mean he was going back. "So?"

"So he offered him the chance to return and he jumped at the opportunity," Cole said, his smile smug, the gleam in his eyes showing his pleasure at the pronouncement.

Her stomach twisted in shock and pain, but she didn't trust Cole. "How would you know this?"

"I went by his office to find out how Damon was feeling, and he was with his friend. They were talking about how much fun they'd had and how they helped people less fortunate. How they were doing good work instead of treating men who earned a fortune and didn't realize how lucky they were."

She narrowed her gaze. "Braden wouldn't say that about people like his brothers."

He might know his athletic limitations, but he didn't resent those who had talent. He wasn't like his father. Like Jesse Prescott.

Cole shrugged. "I just know what I heard. And even if he sticks around, he's going to come to resent this life when he could be free to do what makes him happiest."

"You know what? You're an asshole." She walked away, her shoulder bumping against his as she passed.

"You just don't want to face the truth," he called out to her as she strode to her office, ignoring him despite the fact that her pulse was pounding too hard to be healthy.

She reached her space and was about to close herself inside so she could think when Steffy slipped in behind her. "Hey, friend!"

"Hi." Willow slid down onto her chair.

"What's wrong?" Steffy plopped into a seat of her own.

Still trying to make sense of what had just happened, Willow said, "Cole claims Braden's friend from

Doctors Without Borders came by, asked him to return, and he said yes."

"Do you believe him?" Steffy leaned her elbows on the desk. "Because the guy I've seen the last few weeks wouldn't go anywhere without you."

Willow placed her hand over her pounding heart, her head torn between what Steffy said and she wanted to believe and what Cole claimed to have overheard.

For the first time in her life, she listened to her heart. If she didn't, she would have no future, no life, no possibility of happiness. Braden hadn't spent all his time trying to show her how he felt just to run back to Brazil. He had too much to live for here. His family, the new job, the clinic that he loved ... and her if she'd just tell him how she really felt about him.

"No. I don't believe him."

She trusted Braden. But that didn't mean she could let it go without finding out what had really happened. And she also needed to ask him the one question she'd been holding inside her.

"Good because he's a jealous prick," Steffy said.

Willow managed a laugh. "I need to talk to Braden," she said, pushing herself up from her seat.

"I saw him leave with his sister. I think they were going for lunch." Steffy stood. "Let's go get something to eat, too, okay? You can talk to him when you get back."

She paused and shook her head. "Before I see Braden, there's one stop I need to make. Someone I need to talk to."

Steffy shrugged. "Suit yourself. I'm going to get a taco."

Willow burst out laughing. "Of course you are."

Steffy waved as she started to head out. "Be nice and I'll bring one home for you."

"Would you? Please?"

Pausing at the door, Steffy smiled. "Sure thing. And wherever you're going, good luck."

Chapter Thirteen

WILLOW PULLED UP to Bella's house, surprising herself, because in the past, if she'd gotten news like Cole had just dropped on her, she'd have not only believed it, she'd have run far and fast before Braden could hurt her by leaving first. She wouldn't turn to anyone. Trust anyone. But here she was at the home of the woman who'd taken her in and treated her like family.

She strode up the bluestone steps leading to the front entrance and rang the bell.

Bella answered, the shock on her face evident. "Willow! Aren't you usually at work? Honey, is everything okay?" she asked, pushing open the door and letting her inside.

"I'm okay. I just needed your wise advice. Can we sit in the family room?" Willow asked.

"Of course."

Once they settled on the floral sofa that hadn't changed since Willow walked into this home for the first time, Bella studied her. "Talk to me."

After drawing a deep breath, Willow let it out and

spoke. "I think I'm in love with Braden." Her heart rate sped up at the admission, something she hadn't even felt when they were together before. It had been impossible with her holding so much of herself back. And if she thought the pain of losing him had been bad two years ago, she couldn't imagine the magnitude of the feelings if it happened again.

"You think or you know?" Bella's wise gaze met hers.

Willow's lips twisted in a wry smile. "I know. I'm just petrified." She twisted her hands together in her lap, well aware of the nerves spiraling through her body.

"Does he love you? Has he said?"

She shook her head. "His actions make me think he does." And the experience of his body inside hers was so much more intense now than it had been then. He was everything to her.

"So what's wrong? I don't think you're here just because you're afraid you fell in love."

"No." Willow thought back to her conversation with Cole and explained what he'd told her to Bella and how she didn't want to believe him. "And what if Braden is actually leaving again?" The thought made her nauseous.

"What if he isn't? What if your gut feeling is right and Cole is stirring up trouble? Then you are going to be in the position of having to open up to your man eventually. Admit your feelings and see if they're reciprocated."

And risk the possibility that they weren't. That Braden cared for her and was having fun but he wasn't thinking about a long-term future with her. The little girl inside her used to being abandoned screamed *no* with absolute certainty. She couldn't put herself out there.

Bella placed a hand on Willow's, and she found the touch comforting. "Just think about how he makes you feel. Then see if you can work on your trust issues a bit. If not, you might miss out on the love of a lifetime."

Willow glanced up at Bella, surprised. "How can you be so optimistic after all you've just been through?" Her husband, his criminal actions, lies, and deceit.

She shrugged, reaching out and gently tucking a strand of Willow's hair behind her ear. "Because it's better than being negative and thinking there's no hope left in my life. Now granted, I didn't grow up the way you did, but I'd like to think you were with me long enough to have felt love, learned to accept it, and give it back?"

Embarrassed, she couldn't meet the other woman's gaze. "You know, up until two years ago, I would have said no. That I hadn't learned." She shook her head and a tear she hadn't expected fell down her face. "Up until a few weeks ago even, I didn't feel that way. But…" She hesitated, wondering how to explain her change of heart.

"But here you are, seeking advice because you realize when you needed someone I've always been here?"

Willow smiled and looked at the woman she did truly love and who'd given her so much. "Yes. Exactly."

"Which means you've opened your heart and learned to trust. Now can you give Braden the same chance?" Bella's sweet, caring voice did its job.

As did all the work Braden had put into their relationship since he'd been back. He'd come home changed in a lot of ways, and though she hadn't wanted to see him for the man he'd become then, she did now.

Reaching over, she pulled Bella into a hug. "Thank you so much."

Bella embraced her and pulled back. "All I did was give you a nudge in the right direction," she said with a smile.

"No, I mean thank you for being there. For taking me in, for giving me a life … and for keeping me in your family."

Bella had taught her how to open her heart, just

like she'd said. And as Bella had been there for Willow, Willow had recently done the same for Aurora. And there was no way the young woman wasn't part of Willow's family forever, too. So she'd learned from Bella and acted without even realizing it.

"And now? What's your plan?" Bella asked.

"I'm going to go get my man." Willow had to believe Braden was waiting for her to say the words first, probably because if he'd said them, he feared she might freak out.

Well, no longer.

She was through giving in to her fear and letting her past rule her present and ruin her future.

*   *   *

BRADEN HAD A great lunch with Bri. His sister, so much fun and full of spunk and life, never failed to make him laugh. While eating, they'd talked mostly about Damon's injury, Dare Nation and his potential role there, and their concern about their brother. Then there was the recent news his mom had shared. She'd broken up with her boyfriend and was dating again, which was always interesting for them to deal with.

They walked out of the deli together, him carrying a turkey, lettuce, tomato, and mayo sandwich with a side of well-done French fries, the way Willow liked them.

Carly Phillips

He blinked into the glare of the hot sun and cursed because he'd left his sunglasses in the car.

"So this is it? Willow's the one?" Bri asked. "Because I've never seen you so happy or settled, even," she said as they approached their vehicles parked side by side so Bri could head back to Dare Nation and Braden to the stadium.

"If I have my way, yes. I've been giving her space to come to terms with her past and my dick move of leaving her last time we were together." But he was getting restless keeping things light. He wanted her to know how he felt about her and move their relationship along.

Bri nodded. "Well, since she's good for you, I approve," she said with a smile.

"Good because I bought a ring."

Bri froze. "You what?"

He grinned. "I bought a ring for Willow that I have stashed in a safe in my apartment."

Her smiled grew wide. "Well, damn, brother, you move fast!"

He shrugged. "I learned my lesson losing her once. I'm not doing it again."

She adjusted her sunglasses on her face and nodded. "Well, I'm in your corner. But I'm sweating, so I'm going to say goodbye and get into my air-conditioned car." She leaned up and kissed his cheek.

"Take care and talk soon. And good luck!"

"Bye, Bri." He turned and unlocked his vehicle, like Bri, anxious to cool off.

Twenty minutes later, he walked back into the stadium and immediately went in search of Willow. Not only did he have lunch for her, he had news he wanted to share about both the clinic and Adam's return and Braden's reply. Telling her he'd turned the man down would go a long way toward reassuring her about his intentions to stick around permanently.

When he didn't find her in her office, he headed for the training room. There were a variety of trainers and therapists working on their patients but no Willow.

He turned and bumped into Cole. Fucking guy was always around. "What now?" he asked him.

"Just wondered if you were looking for Willow?"

Braden narrowed his gaze. "First you're always up my ass and now you're digging into my relationship. Why?" He was through with this asshole but had to play it cool in public.

"Just trying to do you a solid. I saw her and let her know you'd met with your Doctors Without Borders pal and agreed to go back."

"Excuse me?" Braden's heart raced as panic set in. "Why the fuck would you lie?" He shook his head. "Never mind. Stupid question."

Cole smirked and Braden wanted to punch the smile off his self-satisfied face.

"I made sure to tell her you two reminisced about your time in Brazil and how much you preferred helping the less fortunate than wealthy athletes who had it all. That going back was a no-brainer. She ran out of here fast." He rocked on his heels, laughing at Braden's shocked expression.

Gritting his teeth, Braden stepped into his space, and since he towered over the man, Cole shrank back.

"You're a dick and you'll be out of a job if I have anything to say about it. But I don't have the time or patience to deal with you now." Braden elbowed past Cole, deliberately shoving him aside.

He needed to talk to Willow. After he secured the most important part of his life and made sure she knew Cole Walsh was a fucking liar, then he'd talk to Ian about getting rid of the trash.

Cole's laughter echoed in his ear as Braden made his way to his office. Slamming his door shut, he tossed the bag of food onto the desk and pulled his phone out of his pocket, hitting Willow's name, which was the first on his list of important contacts.

The phone rang, rang, and went to voicemail. "Shit."

Leaving everything behind, including lunch, he headed back to his car and drove directly to Willow's apartment, panicking the entire time. If Cole had worked on her insecurities and she'd believed his lies because she was vulnerable, he'd have to work hard to regain her trust all over again.

He pulled into a spot and glanced around the parking lot, but he didn't see her car. Resting his head on the top of the wheel, he groaned. Just in case, he went up to her apartment.

Aurora answered his knock. "Braden, hi!" Aurora met him with a happy smile. "Come in!"

He stepped into the apartment and saw Linc Kingston zipping up a huge suitcase he'd obviously bought for Aurora. "You're leaving?" Braden asked.

She nodded. "I told Willow this morning and promised we'd have dinner tonight. She was supposed to invite you."

He didn't want to worry her. "We've both been busy all day. I didn't get a chance to talk to her yet. But she left early and I thought maybe she came home?"

Aurora shook her head. "I haven't seen her. She usually works all day, though." She glanced at him, confusion in her eyes because, yeah, he ought to know that.

"Thanks. I was just playing a hunch. I'll see you for dinner tonight," he promised. "I won't miss my chance to say goodbye," he said, smiling at her. He turned his gaze to the other man, watching him in silence. "You'll take good care of her," he said, more a demand than a question.

Linc straightened his shoulders. "I should be insulted you'd have to say it, but I'm glad you're looking out for her, too."

"Hello, I'm right here." Aurora waved her hands in the air. "No need to talk around me and about me," she said, showing she was astute as well as smart and causing both Braden and Linc to laugh at their own posturing.

"Okay, I need to get going. I'll see you tonight." Braden turned to Linc. "Will you and Jordan join us?"

"I didn't want to intrude but yes. I'd like to get to know the people in Aurora's life." Linc extended his hand and Braden shook it.

He said goodbye and walked back to his car, at a loss as to where he could find Willow. He headed home, his thoughts scattered and preoccupied as he pulled into his parking lot, cut the engine, and stepped out of his vehicle.

Shoving his keys into his pocket, he strode toward the building entrance.

"Braden!"

He turned at the sound of his name and saw Willow walking toward him. He'd been so in his own head he hadn't noticed her car parked nearby.

With sunglasses on, he couldn't read the message

in her eyes or her expression. But she was here, looking gorgeous as ever in her black stretch pants and body-hugging Thunder shirt.

"Hey!" He met up with her in the middle of the parking lot. Needing to touch her, he braced his hands on her waist.

"Hi." Her lips lifted but the worried smile did little to ease the churning in his gut.

Everything he wanted stood right in front of him, and he had no idea if one jealous asshole's attempt at digging into her insecurities and undermining their relationship had worked.

*   *   *

WILLOW STARED INTO Braden's eyes. Concern was etched in the small lines around his mouth, and his grip on her waist tightened as if he feared her bolting at any moment.

"What's going on?" She knew what her issues were thanks to Cole, but Braden obviously had something on his mind, as well.

A bead of sweat dripped down one side of his face, and he swiped at it with one hand. "Let's go inside and talk. It's too hot out here."

She nodded, letting him slip his hand into hers as they headed into the building and up to his apartment. She appreciated the cool air that surrounded her as she stepped over the entry.

No sooner had he shut the door behind them than he turned to her, eyes blazing. "I didn't tell Adam I'd go back to Brazil. I'm not rejoining Doctors Without Borders, Cole Walsh is a fucking liar, and I love you."

She couldn't control her smile. "I know, I know, you're so right, and I love you, too."

He blinked in surprise. "Wait. What?"

She laughed at the rightness of the moment and laced her fingers behind his neck. "I think you heard me correctly."

He tipped his head to the side. "Cole told you Adam came by and asked me to return, right?"

She nodded. "He did."

"The bastard was listening at my open door. But I turned Adam down. I never considered saying yes. Not for a second. Are you saying you didn't believe him?"

She pulled in a deep breath and opted for honesty. "I admit I panicked … at first."

He slid his arms around her waist and pulled her close. "I totally understand."

"But then I caught myself and realized that I was selling you short. Selling us short. Because you've done nothing but prove to me how you feel. How much you care. And how much you've changed. You aren't the same man who walked out just like I'm not the same woman who just let you go, either."

His grasp tightened. "You need to know that, at the time, I wasn't thinking of it as leaving you."

She pulled in a sharp breath. This was it. The moment she'd pushed away because she'd been afraid of the answer. "What *were* you thinking?"

"C'mere." He guided her over to the sofa and sat down, pulling her onto his lap.

She cuddled in close, soaking in his heat and strength, so glad she'd pushed past her fears to get *here*.

"See, I don't think I ever realized how much *my* past, my childhood, impacted me," Braden said. He twirled a strand of her hair around his finger as he spoke. "I grew up surrounded by talented, athletic siblings, and here I was, the brainiac of the family, who certainly didn't make my father proud."

She stiffened, hating that anyone made him feel less than the perfect. "I'm so sorry."

"It is what it is … or should I say it was what it was? But when Hudson came to me and offered the opportunity to go with him, all I could think about was, *this is it. My chance to carve out a place for myself in the world apart from my family*, and I took it."

She nodded in understanding. Not once since that time had she thought of his reasons for taking the position and leaving everyone he loved behind. She'd been so wrapped up in her own head and past, she hadn't given a thought to him or his emotional needs.

"Selfish," she muttered. "I was so selfish. I should have been worried about you. Instead I was tied up with me."

He shook his head. "Shh. We both handled it not in the best way. And I admit I thought I'd go, and we'd somehow manage to stay together, but that was naïve and stupid. I didn't take your past or your feelings into consideration."

"And I didn't let you explain or discuss it with me. I cut you off and walked away." She brushed his hair off his forehead. "I'm sorry."

"Don't be. To be honest, I don't think I understood the job until I got there. After I saw the good I was accomplishing, I realized my calling to be a doctor wasn't something to be made fun of, like my father did, but that I could make a difference. Without a football," he said wryly. "It got me over my so-called daddy issues."

She appreciated his honesty and the vulnerability he showed her and needed to reciprocate. "Can I ask you something?"

He brushed his lips over hers. "Anything."

She rested her hand on his chest, over his heart. "Was it easy to leave me?" she asked. Because that was her biggest fear. That she was disposable. Easy to leave, to abandon.

Grasping her wrist, he intertwined their fingers. "No. Leaving you was the hardest part of what I did. I thought about you all the time. And I can honestly promise you, I won't be going anywhere without you again."

He stretched out on the sofa, pulling her on top of him, his mouth devouring hers in all the best ways, and as kissing turned to stripping each other out of their clothes and their bodies finally joining together, Willow knew she'd found her home at last.

They lay in blissful silence for a few minutes when a nagging thought began to intrude. "I hate to ruin the mood, but I have to ask. What are you going to do about Cole and the fact that he tried to manipulate us into breaking up?"

He let out a low, annoyed growl at the mention of her ex. "I'm talking to Ian as soon as I can find him about firing the son of a bitch. I can't have someone working under me that I don't trust. Not to mention I don't want the bastard around you anymore."

Her shoulders relaxed at his words. "Good. I never realized how devious or jealous he could be."

"He hid it well. But don't give him another thought. He's not our problem anymore or won't be very soon."

Eventually, they moved into the bedroom, and she settled beneath the covers, the air conditioning chilling her skin.

"I'll be right back," Braden said, striding naked toward the bathroom, giving her a titillating view of his tanned back and firm behind, but she realized he'd walked into the closet instead.

She shrugged and lay back against the pillows, closing her eyes, feeling when his weight dipped the mattress. She pushed herself up against the pillows. Noticing he had one hand behind his back, she wrinkled her nose in confusion. "What do you have there?"

He drew in a deep breath. "I may be getting ahead of myself here, but the one thing that's been between us is your questioning my commitment to you. Whether or not I'd stay in town."

"A fear I think I proved to you I've conquered." And she was proud of that fact.

He nodded. "But that doesn't change what I want for us. For my future. For *our* future." He moved his arm from behind his back and revealed a small black velvet ring box, and she sucked in a startled breath.

"Braden?"

"I bought this knowing what I wanted but realizing I had to give you time to trust me, and I know now that you do." He opened the box to reveal an emerald-cut diamond halo setting in a white-gold band with smaller diamonds making up the ring.

"Willow, I love you now and I will love you for the rest of my life. I don't want to rush you into anything you aren't ready for as far as how soon we get married, but I hope you'll agree to wear my ring. And marry me when you're ready."

She stared at the gorgeous ring, tears in her eyes. Not too big, not tiny, it was just perfect for her to wear every day, and he obviously knew it. "It's so beautiful."

Never in her wildest dreams had she imagined him wanting to marry her and give her everything she wanted in life. A family and a future together. Something she'd never believed she'd have as she'd been passed from one set of foster parents to another. Until she'd found Bella. And now Braden. All it had taken was opening herself up and allowing herself to see what was in front of her.

She looked up and met his nervous gaze, realizing she was making the poor man wait for an answer. "Yes, I'll marry you," she said with a grin. "A million times yes."

"Thank God." He took her hand in his, slipping the engagement ring on her left third finger before sealing his lips over hers for a long, long, wet kiss.

He lifted his head and pulled her into his arms.

"If it's okay with you, I don't want to wait to get married." Now that she was all in, she wanted everything. "I can't wait to start our lives together."

He squeezed her tighter against him. "Yeah? Well, then it won't freak you out to know I've been looking online at houses for us."

She sighed, glad he wanted to move as quickly as she did. "It doesn't freak me out at all."

"You know we can't just elope. My family would kill us."

She laughed. "I know that. I just want to plan and not put it off."

Stretching them out on the bed, he wrapped his arms around her and pressed his lips to her neck. "I'm ready when you are."

"Good." Because after hiding her feelings and emotions for so long, she'd found her home with Braden, and she never wanted to let him go.

Epilogue

BRADEN AND WILLOW told Aurora about their engagement at her goodbye dinner that same night. They'd met up early so she and Linc could fly home at a decent hour. Aurora was so excited, she begged them to wait to get married until she could travel with the baby, and how could they say no to that?

Saying goodbye to her was bittersweet for them both but mostly for Willow, who'd grown to think of her as a sister in a very short time. Linc promised to take good care of her, and Aurora swore she'd stay in touch, while Braden and Willow promised to come visit when the baby was born.

Willow didn't want to take her ring off, and they couldn't just have Damon and everyone find out by accident, so after saying goodbye to Aurora and Linc, they headed directly over to Braden's mom's house to announce the news. Christine Prescott cried as she welcomed Willow to the family, and within thirty minutes, calls had been made to all the siblings, bringing Braden's family up to speed.

From there, they stopped at Bella's place. She was the closest thing Willow had to a mother, and, as Willow had explained, she'd played a role in convincing Willow to be up-front and honest about her feelings for Braden. Once everyone close to them knew, they were able to go back to Braden's for a private celebration of their own.

The next few months passed quickly. First the Miami Thunder won the Super Bowl without Cole Walsh, who Ian had allowed Braden the pleasure of firing for cause, and with Damon on the sidelines. He'd waited for the season to come to an end before announcing his retirement for medical reasons and informing the press he'd be joining Dare Nation, where he'd shadow Austin while learning the ropes. Meanwhile, Braden was giving Hudson the time he needed to work out his part of the financing for the clinic.

Aurora, they'd learned via FaceTime, calls, and texts, had adapted well to her new family, and soon after, she gave birth to a baby girl. Braden and Willow had flown to New York to visit, and it had been obvious she was flourishing under the Kingstons' love and care.

On a warm February fourteenth, Valentine's Day, Austin and Quinn's wedding day arrived. They'd ended up booking a large hotel ballroom for the event because between Austin's huge family and Quinn's many cousins, they had many more guests than originally intended.

Before the ceremony, gathered in the room were all the Prescott brothers, Uncle Paul and Ron, and Hudson. The space was tight, but no one seemed to care because this was one of the few times they'd all been together and alone since pairing up and creating their own lives.

Bri was in the bridal suite with Quinn and baby Jenny – Austin and Quinn's daughter, or she would be Quinn's since they were signing adoption papers today, as well. Also with them were Christine, Bella, Macy, Evie, Quinn's mom, and the other females in her large family.

"I'd like to make a toast," Austin said, picking up the glass of scotch. An expensive bottle had been left in the room along with appetizers. "Does everyone have a glass?"

"Yep." Damon lifted his. He'd been adapting well to the new job, dressing in suits, not a uniform, and being around family more often.

"Here, here," Jaxon said, lifting the tumbler with the amber-colored liquid.

"Apple juice," Uncle Paul said in disdain. "Gotta protect that kidney you gave me."

He grinned at Austin, who shook his head and

laughed. "I won't drink much, either, don't worry." With only one kidney, as well, he was extra careful now.

Ron raised his glass. "Sympathy apple juice."

He and Paul had had a solid relationship for so many years, it was one to emulate in any marriage, and Braden took note.

Glancing around at the brothers and men he couldn't imagine his life without, he knew how lucky he was to have them all. Despite the frustrations growing up with a difficult parent, they'd made it through to *this*. They were all married or to be married, in his case, to the women they loved.

Austin cleared his throat. "Many of you beat me to the altar, but remember, I found Quinn before you guys discovered your women."

Braden grinned at the competitive statement, so like each of the brothers.

Austin chuckled, but his expression grew serious. "I feel good getting married knowing you've all discovered the same happiness in your lives. Well, except for you, Hudson." With a joking grin, he glanced at Braden's friend, who was here since, as a bridesmaid, Bri needed a partner to walk her down the aisle, and Hudson was the perfect choice.

Everyone saw the sparks brewing between the two, and putting them together would be fun to watch.

"Thanks for the reminder." Hudson lifted his glass in a mock toast. "But marriage isn't on my radar, and I'm perfectly fine as is."

As far as Braden knew, it wasn't on Bri's, either, so he wasn't worried about her getting hurt if something happened between them. Besides, he trusted Hudson not to break her heart, because if he did, Braden would have to smash his nose, and things wouldn't be pretty. Something Hudson was well aware of.

"You'll find that right person and change your mind," Damon predicted.

"Agreed." This from Jaxon, who then turned to Braden. "When are you and Willow tying the knot?"

They wanted to marry before training camp began in July, which gave them three to four months to plan and execute. Willow didn't want this-sized wedding, not that Braden would insult Austin by saying so. To each their own. But her idea of perfection was just the men in this room, their wives, his sister, Christine, Bella, and her best friend, Steffy.

"We're thinking of pulling a small ceremony together in May sometime. We wanted to wait until Austin and Quinn's ceremony was finished before we picked a date and made it about us." He grinned. "Those were Willow's words."

"Women." Austin shook his head and laughed. "Here's to happiness and the women who complete us."

Short and sweet. So very Austin. None of the Prescott-Dare men, as they'd begun to jokingly call themselves, had thought marriage or monogamy was in their future, but it had taken the right women to change their minds.

A knock sounded on the door. "It's time," someone called out.

Braden glanced at his brother. "You ready?"

"I can't fucking wait."

A few minutes later, they were lined up, their women on their arms. Willow glowed in a cream-colored dress with material that shined, perfectly applied makeup on her face, her beautiful blonde hair curled and falling around her shoulders.

"I can't take my eyes off you," he whispered in her ear, causing her to shiver.

"You're pretty sexy yourself." Her approving gaze took in his attire, a tuxedo and cream-colored bow tie.

And as he leaned close, the scent of her light perfume hit him hard, his body hardening, and he counted backwards to attempt to get rid of his erection.

But the music started, and they had to focus on their walk down the aisle behind the other couples. He glanced around as they stepped slowly and in tandem.

His mother sat beside Paul and Ron, Jenny in her

arms. The baby wore a cream dress she'd spit up on as his mother carried her down the aisle, making everyone laugh. His mother's eyes were filled with happy tears as her children strode down the aisle.

Evie and Damon had already announced her pregnancy, and since she was showing, her bridesmaid's dress had to be adjusted to fit. At least according to Willow.

As Macy and Jaxon passed the crowd, Macy's teenage sister, Hannah, waved from her seat.

He and Willow made their way next. After them, Bri and Hudson walked together, and Braden knew it was only a matter of time before their chemistry either exploded or imploded. Time would tell.

They'd all separated at the end of the aisle, when the women went to stand beside each other, across from the men.

Austin waited for his bride, no nerves, just a huge smile on his face, and when Quinn appeared, looking beautiful in what Willow had informed him would be a white mermaid-style gown, Braden's brother nearly ran forward to grab her and complete the ceremony. Finally Austin and Quinn exchanged vows, promising to love, honor, and cherish each other, and when he kissed the bride, he dipped her low and kept her there for a good long, while, while the crowd whistled.

As happy as Braden was for his brother, all he

wanted was to make Willow his. They'd already found a house in a neighborhood with new construction in Weston and had moved in a couple of weeks ago.

It wasn't enough.

He wanted her to have his name and cement things between them for good.

And in a small ceremony in May, with just family and close friends, he did exactly that.

You met Linc Kingston and his sister Aurora. Order the next book in Carly's new The Kingston Family Series, JUST ONE NIGHT, a friends to lovers, office romance, accidental pregnancy story! PS – The NY Dares and Dare Nation characters will make appearances!

Don't miss out on the newest info on Carly's books! Go HERE to join newsletter and get 2 free books: www.carlyphillips.com/newsletter

About the Author

NY Times, Wall Street Journal, and USA Today Bestseller, Carly Phillips gives her readers Alphalicious heroes to swoon for and romance to set your heart on fire. She married her college sweetheart and lives in Purchase, NY along with her three crazy dogs: two wheaten terriers and a mutant Havanese, who are featured on her Facebook and Instagram. The author of 50 romance novels, she has raised two incredible daughters who put up with having a mom as a full time writer. Carly's book, The Bachelor, was chosen by Kelly Ripa as a romance club pick and was the first romance on a nationally televised bookclub. Carly loves social media and interacting with her readers. Want to keep up with Carly? Sign up for her newsletter and receive TWO FREE books at www.carlyphillips.com.

Made in the USA
Las Vegas, NV
12 June 2022

50143023R00164